PRAISE FOR THE OTHER

Art History Mysteries:

The Bernini Bust

"The cleverest entry yet in this deliciously literate series."
—*Kirkus Reviews*

"As charming as its title—well paced, witty and full of details that speak to his training as an art historian."
—*The San Diego Union-Tribune*

"Art history, literary language and wry humor realize another auspicious combination." —*Library Journal*

The Titian Committee

"Mr. Pears does some lovely brushwork on the minor characters who contribute to the subtle tones of this elegant mystery . . . but the real work of art here is the plot, a piece of structural engineering any artist would envy." —*The New York Times Book Review*

"Light and sassy . . . Agatha would have loved it."
—*Los Angeles Times*

"Writes with a Beerbohm-like wit." —*Publishers Weekly*

Death and Restoration

"Gleeful . . . articulate characters and erudite art commentary . . . high style." —*The New York Times Book Review*

"Pears exhibits quite a masterful touch at suspenseful storytelling . . . [he] writes clearly, persuasively and with a hand guided by touches of sentimentality as well as mischief." —*Chicago Tribune*

"Enjoyable." —*The Washington Post*

"Pears again achieves a delicate, sure balance with a book simultaneously witty and instructive." —*Publishers Weekly*

"An exciting mystery." —*The Dallas Morning News*

continued . . .

"It is to Pears's great credit that the textured paths of modern-day mystery, ancient empires, and religious faith collide so effortlessly. Clearly, his training as both journalist and art historian make for a finely tuned duet. . . . In the end, once all the dots are connected, *Death and Restoration* leaves a memorable, satisfying imprint. We have Pears's subtle technique of mixing intrigue with intelligence to thank for that."
—*The Boston Globe*

"The pleasure of Pears's book . . . lies in its careful . . . revelations of character."
—*The Houston Chronicle*

"Pears's tremendous affection for Rome comes through strongly, making the city one of the most engaging characters."
—*The Sunday Times* (London)

"Pears writes delightfully witty, elegant, well-informed crime novels."
—*The Times* (London)

The Last Judgement

"Clever and entertaining . . . Pears knows what he is talking about and tells a rollicking good yarn."
—*The Boston Globe*

"A sophisticated, adventurous, and gripping story that is sure to hold wide appeal."
—*Booklist*

"The latest (mis)adventure of art historian Jonathan Argyll delivers its plot twists at a rapid clip right up to the closing pages. . . . Pears keeps his readers well occupied."
—*Publishers Weekly*

Giotto's Hand

"Fine art, quirky characters and scenes set in Rome and an English country village add to the joys of *Giotto's Hand*. . . . A neat twist at the end is the cherry on this fudge sundae of a mystery."
—*Minneapolis Star Tribune*

"Pears has a whimsical take on the scruples of the art trade, on English food and plumbing and on Italian bureaucracy . . . A sweet, art world 'cozy.' "
—*The Mercury News* (San Jose)

"Art, crime, and Italy mix well . . . Pears masterfully juggles his plot elements while providing delightful diversion in the contrasting manners of his English and Italian characters."
—*Booklist*

The Art History Mysteries by Iain Pears

THE PORTRAIT
DEATH AND RESTORATION
GIOTTO'S HAND
THE LAST JUDGEMENT
THE BERNINI BUST
THE TITIAN COMMITTEE
THE RAPHAEL AFFAIR

Novels by Iain Pears

THE DREAM OF SCIPIO
AN INSTANCE OF THE FINGERPOST

IAIN PEARS

THE RAPHAEL AFFAIR

BERKLEY PRIME CRIME, NEW YORK

THE BERKLEY PUBLISHING GROUP
Published by the Penguin Group
Penguin Group (USA) Inc.
375 Hudson Street, New York, New York 10014, USA
Penguin Group (Canada), 90 Eglinton Avenue East, Suite 700, Toronto, Ontario M4P 2Y3, Canada
(a division of Pearson Penguin Canada Inc.)
Penguin Books Ltd., 80 Strand, London WC2R 0RL, England
Penguin Group Ireland, 25 St. Stephen's Green, Dublin 2, Ireland (a division of Penguin Books Ltd.)
Penguin Group (Australia), 250 Camberwell Road, Camberwell, Victoria 3124, Australia
(a division of Pearson Australia Group Pty. Ltd.)
Penguin Books India Pvt. Ltd., 11 Community Centre, Panchsheel Park, New Delhi—110 017, India
Penguin Group (NZ), 67 Apollo Drive, Rosedale, North Shore 0632, New Zealand
(a division of Pearson New Zealand Ltd.)
Penguin Books (South Africa) (Pty.) Ltd., 24 Sturdee Avenue, Rosebank, Johannesburg 2196, South Africa

Penguin Books Ltd., Registered Offices: 80 Strand, London WC2R 0RL, England

THE RAPHAEL AFFAIR

A Berkley Prime Crime Book / published by arrangement with the author

PRINTING HISTORY
Harcourt Brace Jovanovich hardcover edition / 1990
Berkley Prime Crime mass-market edition / November 1998
Berkley Prime Crime trade paperback edition / February 2001

ISBN: 978-0-425-17892-8

PRINTED IN THE UNITED STATES OF AMERICA

15 14 13 12 11 10 9 8 7 6 5

To Ruth

Some of the buildings and paintings in this book exist, others do not, and all the characters are imaginary. There is no National Museum in the Borghese Gardens, but there is an Italian art squad in a building in central Rome. However, I have arbitrarily shifted its affiliation from the carabinieri to the polizia, to underline that my account bears no relation to the original.

1

GENERALE Taddeo Bottando walked up the staircase covered in stolen works of art slightly before the bell of San Ignazio struck seven in the morning, as usual. He had turned up in the piazza a good deal earlier but, as was his habit, had passed ten minutes in the bar opposite the office drinking two espresso coffees and eating a *panino* filled with fresh ham. The *habitués* of the bar had greeted him as befitted a regular breakfast customer: a friendly "buon giorno," nods of acknowledgement, but no attempt at any more conversation. Waking up, in Rome as in any other city, is a private matter that is best done in quiet solitude.

That pleasing early morning ritual over, he crossed the cobblestoned piazza and wheezed up the stairs, puffing and blowing heavily before he even finished the first flight. It was not that he was fat, so he reassured himself often. It was years since he'd last needed his military uniform let out. Portly, maybe. Distinguished-looking, he preferred. He should give up cigarettes and coffee and food and take up exercise instead. But what enjoyment would life have to offer then? Besides, he was nearing sixty, and it was too late now to start getting in trim. The effort would probably kill him anyway.

He stopped for a moment, partly to look at a new picture hanging on the wall, but more for a surreptitious opportunity to get his breath back. A little drawing by Gentileschi, by the look of it. Very handsome. Pity it would have to go back to the rightful owners when all the paperwork was done, the culprit charged, and the documentation sent over to the public prosecutor's office. Still, it was one of the compensations of being the chief of the Italian National Art Theft Squad. On the rare occasions when you did recover something, it was generally worthwhile.

"Pretty, isn't it?" a voice said behind him as he peered at the artist's work. Suppressing the last remnants of his breathlessness, he turned round. Flavia di Stefano was one of those wonderful women that Bottando believed only Italy could produce. Either they became wives-and-mothers or they worked. And if they worked, they had to strive so hard to stave off guilt feelings about not staying at home that they were twice as good as anyone else. For that reason eight of the ten researchers were women. This, he knew, had caused his department to win an unfortunate nickname in other parts of the service. But at least Bottando's Brothel, as his obviously jealous colleagues had dubbed his bureau, produced results. Unlike certain others he could mention.

He beamed a benevolent good morning at the girl. Or rather woman; he noted that he was now at an age when any woman under thirty counted as a girl. He liked her a great deal, even though she seemed totally unable to give him the deference to which his rank and age and wisdom entitled him. While some friends referred delicately to his certain roundness, Flavia called him, affectionately and without the least sense of shame, Old Tub. Apart from this, she was an almost perfect junior colleague.

Flavia, who also resolutely insisted on wearing sweaters and jeans to demonstrate that she fell into neither the policewoman nor serious businesswoman category, smiled back at his greeting. It was genuinely meant. In the last few years, the General had taught her an immense amount, mainly by leaving her alone to make mistakes, and covering for her afterwards. He was not one of those employers who see staff as a convenient herd of lambs to be sacrificed whenever something went wrong. Rather, he took immense pride in teaching his charges to do things properly and allowed them considerable, if always unofficial, independence. Flavia, more than most, had responded with enthusiasm and had become a full investigator in everything but name.

"The carabinieri near the Campo dei Fiori rang and

want to bring someone around," she told him. "They arrested him last night breaking into a church on their patch and they say he has an odd story to tell. They seem to think it is more in our line of business."

She spoke in the harsh, nasal accent of the north-west. Bottando had hired her direct from the university at Turin, and she had abandoned a graduate degree to come to Rome. She always maintained that she would finish it eventually, and used this as her main reason for not joining the police fulltime. But she worked so hard in the department that it seemed very unlikely. She had the fair hair and light skin of many northern Italians. Even if she hadn't been simply but definitely beautiful, her hair would have made her stand out in Rome.

"Did they say what it's about?"

"No. Just something about a picture. They reckon he may be a bit crazy."

"What does he speak?"

"English and some Italian. I don't know how much."

"In that case you will have to talk to him. You know what my English is like. Let me know if he has anything interesting to say."

Flavia made a mock salute, two fingers of her left hand pressed briefly against the fringe of meticulously disarranged hair that edged half-way down her forehead. Both of them wandered into their respective offices, she to the small, cramped one she shared with three others, he to the more luxurious one, decorated almost entirely with more stolen objects, on the third floor.

Bottando settled down and went through the morning ritual of going through the mail left on his desk in a neat pile by his secretary. Normal nonsense. He shook his head sadly, sighed heavily, and tipped the entire pile into the bin.

TWO days later, a bulky document awaited him on his desk. It was the fruit of Flavia's interrogations of the prisoner brought round by the carabinieri, and bore all the hallmarks of her conscientiousness. On top of it was a little note: "I think you'll like this one—F." In principle, the interview should have been conducted by a full policeman, but Flavia had swiftly switched into English and gained control of the proceedings. As Bottando flipped through the pages, he realised that the man clearly spoke Italian quite well. But the policeman on duty was fairly dull and probably would have missed almost everything of interest.

The document was a condensed transcript of the interview, the sort of thing that is sent along to the prosecutor's office if the police think a case can be made. Bottando got himself an espresso from the machine in the corridor—he was an addict of many years' standing who now could not even get to sleep at night without a last-minute caffeine fix—put his feet up and began to read.

For the first few pages there was little of any interest. The prisoner was English, aged twenty-eight and a graduate student. He was in Rome on holiday and had been arrested for vagrancy when found apparently trying to sleep in the church of Santa Barbara near the Campo dei Fiori. Nothing had been stolen and no damage reported by the parish priest.

All this took five pages, and Bottando was wondering why his department had been called in and why the carabinieri had bothered arresting him. Sleeping rough was hardly a major offence. Throughout the summer months, foreigners could be found snoring away on almost every bench and in every open space in the city. Sometimes they had no money, sometimes they were too drunk or too drugged to get back to their pensione, just as often there was not an empty hotel room for miles and they had no choice.

But as he flipped over the next page he became more interested. The prisoner, one Jonathan Argyll, informed the interrogators that he had gone to the church not to camp out, but to examine a Raphael over the altar. Moreover, he insisted on making a full statement because an enormous fraud had taken place.

Bottando paused. Raphael? The man clearly was off his head. He couldn't remember the church very well but was convinced that he knew the location of every Raphael in the country. If there was one in a tiny little church like Santa Barbara, he would know about it. He walked to the computer and switched it on. When the machine had hummed and whirred itself into readiness he went into the database that had been built up giving the locations of likely targets for thieves. He typed "Roma," and, when it asked for more details, specified "chiesi." He then typed in the name of the church. The machine instantly told him that Santa Barbara had only six objects that were potentially stealable. Three were bits of silver, one was a seventeenth-century vulgate Bible with an embossed leather binding, and two were pictures. But neither was a Raphael nor likely to be confused with one. Both, in fact, were very second-rate affairs that no thief worth his salt would waste his time stealing. The market for purloined, nine-foot by six-foot crucifixions by anonymous Roman painters was not exactly buoyant. Nor could he see much demand in the illicit international art trade for the altarpiece—a Landscape with the Repose on the Flight to Egypt by the magnificently mediocre eighteenth-century painter Carlo Mantini.

Going back to his desk, he read on for a few more lines, convinced that by "interesting," Flavia merely meant that her document was yet another demonstration of the foolishness of mankind. She was very strong on this interpretation of human nature, especially as far as art collectors were concerned. Several times the department had abandoned the hunt for a minor work when they discovered that it had been bought—as a Michelangelo, Titian, Caravaggio or whatever—by a wealthy foreign collector with more money than sense. To get their revenge they wrote to the buyer informing him that he had been cheated, and passed on word to the local police. But, on the whole, they considered the humiliation the man would suffer was adequate punishment, and generally the work was too unimportant to go to all the trouble and expense of international arrest warrants and deportation orders.

So perhaps this fifty-page document simply catalogued the delusions of an unbalanced moron who had persuaded himself he could get rich quick? A few more glances rapidly persuaded him there was more to it than that. From being a question-and-answer session, the document settled into a sustained narrative, the result of a lengthy statement. Bottando read on, and became more puzzled:

". . . studying for a degree based on a dissertation about Mantini. During my research, I discovered a series of documents that proved beyond any doubt that Mantini earned money by working for art dealers in Rome in the 1720s and had taken part in a sizeable fraud. You mustn't think that Italy's restrictions on exports of works of art are new. Most old states had them even back in the sixteenth century. By the eighteenth century they were becoming onerous. The Papal States in particular were getting poorer, and lots of foreigners were coming here wanting to buy. So, various routes were worked out to bypass the regulations. The most usual was the most obvious: a series of judicious bribes. Pictures were also temporarily reattributed to some obscure painter, until an export licence was given. Occasionally, dealers would go so far as to cut the picture into fragments, ship it to London or Paris, then reassemble and repair it.

"The more important the painting, the more difficult it

was to get it out of the country. I suppose that is also true now. And the most difficult of all were those by—or thought to be by—the great triumvirate of the Renaissance: Raphael, Michelangelo and Leonardo. Several times dealers or collectors bought works by one of these artists, asked the papacy for permission to export, and were turned down. In many cases the pictures are still here. So, when the di Parma family wanted to sell their most valuable possession, something illicit was clearly needed if they were to collect the money.

"The di Parmas had been a great family, one of the most powerful in central Italy. Like many others they had fallen on hard times, and when the Earl of Clomorton offered to buy their Raphael for an outrageous sum they agreed. To get it out of the country, they enlisted the aid of an English art dealer called Samuel Paris, and he turned to Mantini for extra assistance.

"The routine they came up with was beautifully simple. Mantini was to paint over the Raphael and the picture was to leave the country as one of his works. When it got to England the new painting would be cleaned off and the Raphael would take its place in the Earl's collection. Presumably Mantini used a coat of varnish to protect the painting underneath, and used only paint that could be removed easily.

"I don't know any of the details of how it was done technically, but I do know it was done. There is a letter in the Clomorton archives from Paris assuring the Earl that he had watched Mantini apply the paint and seen the

Raphael disappear under its disguise. But Clomorton never hung his picture on his wall.

"At some stage something went wrong, either accidentally or deliberately. The picture must have been switched; the payment for the Raphael was handed over and a different picture was sent to England. Shortly after it arrived, the fraud was evidently discovered and the Earl died. The family doesn't seem to have mentioned the matter again.

"The point is, the Raphael *was* covered by Mantini—this was seen by Paris; it never got to England; and it disappeared from the di Parma collection. On the other hand, the family owned a Mantini in 1728 that they hadn't had four years earlier.

"Now, all of this suggests that the Raphael stayed in Rome under cover. If that was the case, I don't know why they never wiped the disguise off. But they didn't, the Mantini stayed in the collection and was evidently considered to be of such small importance that in the 1860s they donated it to Santa Barbara as an altarpiece.

"And there you are. The picture has rested unknown in that church for more than a century. I first saw it a year ago when I was working on my dissertation. Then I decided a Raphael may be underneath, came back to check, and it's gone. Someone has pinched the damn thing."

EVEN when seen through the stilted prose of an official document, the prisoner's sense of outrage was clear. Not only had he been jilted out of one of the most remarkable art discoveries of the decade, he had got himself arrested as a vagrant to boot. If, indeed, it *was* a remarkable discovery. Either way, if the painting had vanished, it was something to look into. Seeing an excuse for a stroll, he summoned Flavia, walked down the stairs, and set off for Santa Barbara.

ONE of the delights of his job, so Bottando thought to himself as they walked, was the chance of living in Rome. Although not born here, he considered himself very much a Roman and had spent most of the past thirty years in the city. Much of his dislike of his previous assignment in Milan had been prompted not by the job, but because he had had to live in a city which he regarded as soulless and drab.

Then came his great opportunity. Bottando was summoned back to Rome to combat the growing number of thefts of works of art throughout Italy. The creation of his department was due to the theft of a dozen famous works from one of the best—and theoretically best guarded—museums in the country. The police, as usual, hadn't known where to start. They had no contacts in the art world, didn't know the likely instigators, hadn't a clue what might have happened to the paintings.

In a country where the love of art is part of national identity, the matter quickly bubbled up into a potential scandal once it had been raised. The smaller political parties in the ruling coalition began making speeches about defending the national heritage from rapacious foreigners as a way of irritating the larger group of Christian Democrats. At one stage, it had even seemed as though the socialists would pull out of the coalition, and that love of art would bring down the government—thus giving the country another unusual political first.

But it didn't happen. The polizia, spotting a way of aggrandising itself at the expense of the rival carabinieri, proposed a national task force to combat the problem, and for once were backed up by their minister. And in due course they had chosen Bottando to run it, the call to duty rescuing him from the drudgery of fighting an unequal and losing battle against white-collar criminals and other semi-legitimate hoodlums in the financial waters of central Milan.

His return to Rome had been one of the great joys of his career, and he had spent endless evenings walking the streets, revisiting old and favourite sites like the Imperial remains in the Forum, the quietly confident medieval churches and the extravagant baroque monuments. He was free to wander at his leisure, and blessed the bachelor status which permitted it.

As he and Flavia walked now, he constantly looked around him, and took his assistant on a slightly devious route to their destination. The case they were on was not so urgent that five minutes would make any difference. It was one of those Roman spring mornings which turns the city, for all its traffic jams, noise and untidiness, into a place of magic. The ochre buildings stood out against a clear blue sky, the smells of coffee and food drifted out of bars and restaurants, there was a hum of preparation as the crisp and immaculate waiters set out tables and chairs in small piazzas, talking incessantly as they clipped the fresh white tablecloths in place and arranged flowers in the miniature vases. A few tourists were in evidence, looking tired as usual and dressed in the crumpled clothes and backpacks that were their invariable uniform. But there were not many; the year was too young, and the annual invasion was still several weeks away. For the time being, Rome was for the Romans, and it seemed like very heaven.

The way to their destination lay through the middle of the Campo dei Fiori market. East of this ran the via Giubbonari, a thin, straight lane lined with clothes and shoe shops behind the ruins of Pompey's Theatre. It was far too narrow for any sort of car, but nonetheless several Fiats were wedged halfway down it, horns honking as the pedestrians did their best to make their way past. Just beyond these, in a small passageway on the left that was lined with second-hand booksellers, was Santa Barbara.

It was a tiny church, unvisited even by Bottando. It appeared virtually derelict, and was small enough to look almost like a model. Unlike the great basilicas of the city, this was very much a parish church. Built probably in the seventeenth century, its design was entirely conventional, the sort of thing that even an attentive tourist would pass by without bothering to visit.

The first view of the inside confirmed that the tourist

would probably have been correct in his decision. The ceiling was of plain greyish plasterwork, there were no chapels along the side and the decorations were commonplace. Nonetheless, it still gave Bottando that brief moment, as his body registered the coolness of the interior, his nose caught the faint smell of old incense, and his eyes slowly adjusted to the gloom, that always made him delight in visiting even the most modest of Rome's churches. Like nearly all small churches, there was something sad, neglected, but entirely welcoming about Santa Barbara. The one discordant note was that someone, evidently the priest, had decided to erect a modern altar, which stood out brashly in the old and worn building. Bottando heard Flavia sniff with disapproval.

"Modern priests trying to drum up fresh trade," she commented.

"Maybe," Bottando replied. "I suppose in this area you have to do something. It would be a pity to wake up one day and find that your entire congregation had died of old age."

"I suppose so. But I've never got on with hairy-chested clerical enthusiasm. The intense beady look in their eyes always makes me uncomfortable. Give me corpulent corruption any day."

Bottando began to remark that he would never have thought she was interested in priests. He was trying to push his mind off the subject of his own little paunch, and the worry that this signified decadence in his assistant's mind, when the subject of their discussion came through a small door behind the old altar.

At first sight, he didn't fit the caricature of the tall, gaunt, jesuitical type that Flavia evidently had in mind. He didn't look at all like the sort who spend a few years doing good in the suburbs before rushing off to upset the Pope by running guns in South America. Short, pink and fleshy of face, he seemed more inclined to stay in Rome with a cosy sinecure in the Vatican. But, thought Bottando, you never can tell with priests. At least his greeting when Bottando introduced himself was courteous.

"I gather that you have lost a painting," the policeman began once the preliminary polite noises were over. "As I have been told it might have been stolen, I thought I had better make some enquiries."

The priest frowned, cupping his hands together in front of his stomach in a gesture of clerical thoughtfulness. "I can't imagine who told you that. There used to be an altar painting, true. But we sold it a month or so ago."

"Sold it? To whom? Isn't that church property? I thought these sales normally went through the Vatican. They generally tell us about them."

The priest looked uncomfortable. "Well, it's like this." He paused. "Do you have to make a report or something? I really don't want to get into a bureaucratic muddle over forms and things."

"It all depends. We've been told that a painting here was stolen. The niceties of Vatican routine are not our concern if it wasn't."

"It wasn't." He thought for a moment, then launched into an explanation. "I run a small programme for the addicts who live in the Campo area—food, shelter, some attempts to keep them off drugs, and awake." Bottando nodded and politely encouraged him to get on with it. He had come across dozens of these individual programmes in Milan, generally run by well-meaning priests. As a rule, they didn't even begin to scratch the surface of the problem, but the state provided no better alternative.

"We need a lot of supplies and, as you can see, it's a poor parish. We don't get any donations from visitors, not a penny from the diocese, nothing from the city. About a month ago a man appeared and wanted to buy the altarpiece. He offered enough money to keep the programme going for a year and I took it. The sale wasn't registered with the Vatican because it would have taken most of the money. I decided that my addicts needed it more."

Bottando nodded again. It happened all the time and was understandable, even if it did make his job more difficult. "How much did he pay?" he asked.

"Ten million lire," the priest replied. "I knew all about the painting. It's virtually worthless. I told him so, but he said it was for a collector who wanted a piece by Mantini and was prepared to pay over the odds for it."

"Did he give you a receipt or anything like that?"

"Oh yes, it was all done properly. The deed of sale was even franked properly. If you will wait I'll get it." He hurried back to the sacristy and returned a few moments later with a large piece of white, lined paper with a stamp in the top-right corner. “There,” he said. “Sold, One Reposo by Mantini from the Church of Santa Barbara, Rome, for ten million lire. Dated 15 February and signed by myself and Edward Byrnes, dealer. I see he gave no address. I’d not noticed that before. But he paid me in cash and gave me a donation for the programme as well, so I suppose that doesn’t matter much.”

2

AT about eight that evening, Flavia di Stefano sighed, dumped the remainder of her work, finished and unfinished, in the "out" basket and walked briskly out of the office. It had been a busy day, and not a particularly satisfying one.

After the visit to Santa Barbara, the rest of her day had been taken up with routine enquiries about the Mantini, all of them frustrating for someone who loved finding corruption in high places. Everything about the transaction was entirely legal. The owner had wanted to sell, the buyer had taken the picture to England and had been scrupulous about informing everybody of his intentions. All the forms had been filled in properly, and every legal obstacle with the arts ministry, the treasury and the customs surmounted by the rulebook.

A model of a respectable art dealer in operation. Except that Sir Edward Byrnes, prince of London art dealers, might have been taking a Raphael out rather than some piece of junk. But an afternoon spent combing through the penal code had produced nothing which gave them a case. If Byrnes had painted over the Raphael and concealed the fact, a clear crime. If he had smuggled it out, ditto. If he had stolen it, no trouble. In all those cases they could probably have recovered the picture. But, as far as she could tell, there was nothing against taking out a Raphael covered with a Mantini, if you were not the one who'd put the Mantini over it in the first place. And Byrnes would say he didn't know there was anything special about the picture at all. He'd be lying through his teeth, of course, but nothing could be done about it.

It was annoying. Doubly annoying, in fact. Flavia took it for granted that all art dealers were crooked at some level. Their business, after all, consisted of buying things that they knew the sellers could get more for elsewhere. Byrnes, however, was an absolute model of propriety. Utterly fluent in Italian, he often donated works to Italian museums and lent other pieces for exhibitions. His services in other matters had been rewarded with honours in Italy and France, as well as with his knighthood. By reputation a distinguished and learned man, there was not a trace of his ever having even bent the rules, let alone broken them. It was infuriating and, to Flavia, merely demonstrated that he was too clever to get caught.

It was also annoying because the Italian woman, in this

if not much else, was patriotic. For hundreds of years the rest of the world had picked over Italy and removed its greatest art treasures. Nowhere in Italy now was there a museum that compared with the National Galleries in London or Washington, or the Louvre in Paris. Many paintings only remained in Italy because they were stuck on to the walls, though she had even heard that one American millionaire in the twenties had offered to buy the church in Assisi so that the Giotto frescos decorating it could be shipped back to Arizona. For Italians to lose a Raphael was dreadful, even if they had not even known they had it.

Grumbling thus to herself, Flavia walked quickly along the streets, heading towards the Piazza Navona. She had agreed to meet her erstwhile prisoner for dinner, so she could go over some of the details of his story in an atmosphere that might make him more forthcoming. Not that she thought Argyll had been lying. But an interrogation by the police after a night in the cells often makes people forget little details.

The hurry was because she had almost forgotten. As she walked, she checked her handbag; the strap around her neck, Roman fashion, to guard against pickpockets. There was enough to pay for dinner for two. She had a feeling that her fellow-diner was short of funds, and taking men out to dinner always gave her an agreeable feeling. Her mother would never have gone out with a man on her own. Although she was a liberal sort of mother and countenanced such behaviour in her youngest, the idea of her daughter paying would still have shocked her greatly.

She had arranged to meet her guest at a nearby trattoria. It was not a particularly special one, but near to her apartment, and reliable. Like most Roman eating establishments, it served wonderful pasta, magnificent antipasti and dreadful main courses. Unlike Turin, which really knew what meat was, Romans seemed satisfied with any sort of boot leather. No matter: she was used to it now. But Roman food was still about the only thing that made her nostalgic for her home town.

Argyll was sitting at a table in the corner and waved cautiously at her as she entered. Ordinarily he would have been good-enough looking, in an English sort of way, not that that sort of thing normally appealed much to her. Tallish, fair-haired, conservatively and not very well-dressed by Italian standards. Most remarkable of all, perhaps, were his hands, which were long and delicate. He had wrung them together incessantly during the formal interview. They looked as though they would have been better employed playing the violin, or something. At least, he didn't now seem to be twitching and fiddling so much.

Being freed from temporary incarceration indeed seemed to have done him good, and Flavia remarked on the fact.

"For someone who has just mislaid a Raphael you seem remarkably cheerful," she said.

He beamed at her. "I suppose so. By rights I ought to be dreadfully depressed. On the other hand, of course, the whole business proves I'm right, even though it wasn't quite the type of public acclaim I'd had in mind. Besides which, being arrested by the police is quite interesting, in an odd sort of way."

"They didn't treat you badly, then?"

"Not at all. Charming people. They even let me go out for lunch, as long as I promised to be back in my cell in three hours. I can't see the boys in blue in London operating in quite such a free and easy fashion."

"I imagine that by then they'd decided you weren't a public menace. Didn't the whole business upset you at all, though?"

"Well, yes, it did," Argyll replied, tucking in to his plate of pasta. "It wasn't what I'd imagined at all. I rather saw myself uncovering the picture and making a grand announcement—after warning the parish priest—in some suitably scholarly magazine. Great sensation. Career made, one happy parish priest and the whole world one Raphael the richer."

He was speaking in Italian, which he spoke with some fluency. Not perfect by any means, and heavily accented, but more than acceptable. Flavia always believed in speaking Italian to foreigners if possible. Not many of them could, and those who tried could usually only manage phrases culled from guidebooks and street signs, but she felt she should make them practise. She herself had spent years learning English, and saw no reason why others shouldn't make a similar effort.

"But now we have one very unhappy parish priest, an

even more unhappy Vatican, Byrnes with the picture, and your career very far from made," she pointed out. "You're sure that there's something under it?"

"I wasn't at all sure, that's why I wasted so much money to come here and check. It took me months to get enough to buy the ticket. And I couldn't check it because it wasn't there any more. I was just standing around wondering what to do next. And before I could make up my mind, those flatfooted policemen of yours saw the door was open and collared me. But," he added, "I'm sure there is now. Someone like Byrnes wouldn't pull off a stunt like this unless he knew it was worthwhile."

"What I don't understand is why you didn't just write to the priest months ago, tell him your idea, and get permission to have the painting examined. Then he wouldn't have sold it until it had all been cleared up."

"Oh, that's simple. I'm an idiot. And an apprentice academic as well, which is worse." Argyll looked gloomy, put his fork down, the idea clearly having made him lose his appetite. "Art history, as you probably know, is a nasty, vicious profession. I reckoned that if I said a word to anyone in Italy, some big shot in the Museo Nazionale would get there first and take the credit. That's happened before, and who could resist the temptation? It would've been the greatest find for years."

"It still will be," added Flavia a little unnecessarily, dealing a further savage blow to his appetite.

"Thank you," he replied.

Flavia looked at him sympathetically. By all accounts

all he'd wanted was a little bit of fame, a small boost to a career in a desperately overcrowded profession. And even that had been snatched from his grasp by Byrnes's desperate desire for even more money than he already had. "Can't you just write the article anyway? And why tell Byrnes in the first place? You haven't exactly been playing the master tactician through all this, but *that* seems the daftest course you could possibly have taken."

"I didn't tell him," Argyll said indignantly. "I may be dim, but I'm not that bad. I haven't told a soul. Well, except my supervisor. I had to tell him. But he's awfully discreet, hates art dealers and has been incommunicado in Tuscany ever since. Can't possibly have been Tramerton. Nice man really," he continued, going off at a conversational tangent. "I suppose I should send him a letter about all this. Going to jail to forward historical knowledge should impress even him.

"As for my article . . . Well, I will write one. But I'll have to do something a bit faster to stake my claim. It takes months to get a piece in a decent journal. By the time it came out, everybody would be sick of hearing about bloody Raphael. The moment Byrnes is sure he's got the right picture, the press will be called in. Sensational discovery, the works. His tame academics will write glowing articles about translucent masterpieces. And when the enthusiasm reaches its peak, the damn thing will move to Christie's."

Argyll paused as the waiter brought the next course, which he looked at with distaste. "And every museum, every loony millionaire in the world, will be there to bid," he went on. "Something like the Getty would mortgage its grandmother to have it. Can you imagine what sort of price it will fetch? It will make a bunch of sunflowers by Van Gogh seem bargain basement."

"Why so much? It's not as if Raphaels are thin on the ground. He churned out dozens of pictures."

"I know, and they're all in museums or painted on the walls of the Vatican. There hasn't been a real one on the market for decades. Let alone a new one discovered. It's all supply and demand. Even if it doesn't turn out to be very good, it'll still fetch a fortune. Especially with a story like this attached to it."

"Not a bad return on a ten million-lire investment."

"That's what he paid?" Argyll paused to consider the iniquities of the world. "That makes it even worse. Even I could have raised that much. Well, almost, anyway."

He had a well developed, if somewhat morbid, sense of humour, Flavia noted. He was also self-deprecating and appeared to be intelligent, despite apparently deliberate attempts to hide the fact. From being a simple business venture, the meal was turning into a moderately enjoyable occasion.

"Tell me," began her guest in an ostentatious attempt to change the subject, and demonstrate that he wasn't entirely obsessed with errant masterpieces, "What's your job like? Plenty of work? Job satisfaction?"

She grimaced. "Certainly plenty of work. It's like living under a permanent avalanche. Someone or other calculated that one work disappears every ten minutes. It's amazing there's anything left to steal."

Argyll observed that, so far, Italy seemed to have plenty left.

"That's just the trouble. There seems to be an almost infinite amount kept in tumbledown country churches and half-abandoned houses. It keeps vanishing, and often as not the thefts aren't even reported."

Argyll discovered to his delight that Flavia smoked, so fished out his own crumpled packet and lit up. "Why not? What's the objection to reporting a theft?"

She counted the points off on her fingers as she spoke. "One: basic distrust of the police. Two: conviction that we won't get it back anyway. Three: desire to stop the authorities knowing what else they have in case it gets taxed. Four: threats. What do you think? If I had to choose between a painting and my ears, I think I'd also choose to wave goodbye to the painting."

It was not a bad evening. Argyll listened with every appearance of genuine interest in what she had to say, which made a nice change from the usual sort of meal where she was expected to listen with open-mouthed admiration as her date for the evening demonstrated his great qualities. He also had a fund of miscellaneous anecdotes and kept his end of the conversation going. There was only one minor incident after she had paid the bill in the restaurant when, with his hands between his knees, and rocking forward and backward slightly in an agonised fit of embarrassment, Argyll had squinted at the ceiling and said, "I don't suppose . . ." and then paused, and smiled foolishly.

By Italian standards it scarcely counted as an advance: one ardent suitor had only been stopped when Flavia smacked him in the face with a handy frying pan. But she had met enough Englishmen to realise what was intended, even if the technique was so reticent as to make the suggestion almost unnoticeable. Fortunately, dealing with the problem was easy: she had smiled back, and suggested an ice-cream. It seemed to be a more than suitable alternative, and the offer was accepted with evident relief.

They finished off the evening by taking a turn twice round the Piazza Montecitorio before heading for Giolitti's. Flavia was Italian and Argyll had spent enough time in the country to accept that a day without an ice-cream was a day wasted. And slowly eating it while walking the streets along with the rest of the population was a good way of restoring faith that the world was an essentially benevolent place, despite all the recent evidence to the contrary.

3

ARGYLL swung in through a door in the via Condotti and mounted the stairs. He walked quickly past the janitor at the bottom, waving in a familiar sort of style. He should, properly, have shown the card which proved he was entitled to visit Rome's foreign press club. As he didn't have one, that was difficult. Janitors in Rome, anyway, don't often care too much about minor details.

He headed for the bar, an unattractive, tubular steel and artificial wood affair, sat down and ordered an aperitif. Then he looked around and spotted his quarry. Rudolf Beckett could be seen in the next room, alone at a table, eating a late lunch. A large glass of whisky rested in front of him. Argyll walked over and sat down.

"Jonathan. What brings you back to Rome?" Beckett thumped him on the shoulder with one hand, and shook his hand vigorously with the other. He had become one of Argyll's closest friends during his stay in Rome a year or so back. They had run into each other at a minor diplomatic party on the via Giulia. Both had felt out of place, so had naturally spent much of the evening drinking their host's alcohol and being rude about the guests. Afterwards they had gone on to a bar near by and drunk some more. It had cemented the friendship.

Not that they had anything in common. Argyll was a quiet and somewhat introverted Englishman, Beckett an aggressive workaholic with a permanent shake derived from too much drink, too little sleep, and all-consuming neuroses about the next story, the next cheque and whether anybody really liked him. As Argyll clearly did, he had never borne the brunt of one of the tumultuous outbursts of rage that made Beckett's colleagues a little wary of his company.

"Wild geese," he replied to the greeting. "I've just been let out of jail."

Beckett suppressed a smirk.

"No jokes, please," he continued, to head off the quip that the journalist was obviously on the verge of uttering. "I'm not resilient enough yet. I was wondering if you wanted a nice story."

"Is the Pope Catholic? Course I do. Depending on what it is. As long as you remember I can't pay anything for it."

"I don't want anything like that. To see it in print would be enough."

Argyll then retold the story of his discovery and the incursion of Sir Edward Byrnes, ending with his night in the cell. "My discovery. Pinched. Just like that. Could you write something so everyone knows what really happened? Otherwise Byrnes will get all the credit as well as all the money."

"Nice story," commented Beckett, finishing off another whisky and moving straight on to a large grappa. "But the lead is the Raphael, not your being diddled. However, an expert hack like myself will be able to do it. Great discovery, famous artist, etc., etc. Then a bit of stuff about you further down, undermining the whole thing and making Byrnes out to be a proper toad. Easy.

"You'll forgive me, though, but I must check up on the story first. A few phone calls, here and there, that sort of thing. OK? Feel better? You don't look as though you've been greatly enjoying the eternal city."

"I haven't. The only good thing that's happened so far has been having dinner with that policewoman last night . . ."

"That does sound bad."

"Not at all. She's very lovely. Remarkably lovely, in fact. As I've got to go back to London tomorrow, it doesn't really matter, though."

AS Beckett explained in a letter a few weeks later, it wasn't really his fault, and he sent his original article to prove it. He had written the story as promised: revelation about a possible new Raphael, attributed to "museum sources"; a quotation of cautious optimism from Byrnes, a few comments from a couple of art historians, then some quite well-researched background about other remarkable discoveries in the past few years. From there on, Beckett had written about Argyll and had clearly and concisely got the message across. Young graduate student cheated by machinations of sly dealer. It didn't actually say that, of course, but the general implication was crystal clear. It was a good article.

Unfortunately, it was a bit too good. He had sent it off to the editor of his paper in New York and this man had been excited by it. So it had gone on the front page, left side, single column, instead of in the arts section as Beckett had expected. But it was a busy time of year. A summit meeting was in the offing, another bribery and corruption scandal had broken out among local politicians, the administration was indulging in another spate of Libya-bashing. The editor hadn't wanted to run the story over on to an inside page. So he made it fit by cutting it down a bit, and had sliced off the bottom seven paragraphs. With these went all mention of Argyll.

In every other respect, the article worked wonders, and stimulated enormous public interest. Over the next few months, all of Argyll's predictions to Flavia about the Raphael came true. The story of the eighteenth-century fraud and its discovery captured the imagination. Both the *New York Times Magazine* and the arts supplement of the

London *Observer* duly carried lengthy accounts of the art-historical detective work which had led to the pot of gold. They, also, neglected to mention Argyll, but were otherwise solidly written. Byrnes's sales campaign was well under way.

Argyll indulged his sense of mild masochism by collecting the articles. All sorts of critics and historians invaded what he had previously considered to be his turf. The diligent research of others produced dozens of little fragments to complete his partial picture and show the results of his haste. One article reproduced letters from the Earl's brother-in-law indicating he had died of a heart attack from shock at the fraud, and that the family had covered up their loss for fear of embarrassment: "Rest assured, dear sister, no fault attaches to you for the attack. Such an event was entirely due to his own injudicious choice and hasty character. But these matters will remain between us alone; the disgrace to our family, and the scorn of certain of our friends could not be tolerated . . ." That particularly outraged him. He had seen the same letter, but had decided it was inconclusive. Now everything else was clear, so was the letter.

What was worse was that all these little articles meant that even the modest piece he had planned for the *Burlington Magazine* was not possible; everything had already been published at least once. He avoided his friends and found a peculiar form of solace in going back to the *Life and Times of Carlo Mantini, 1675–1729*. At least he could finish that. It wouldn't be so good now that one of his central chapters had become about as original as the plot of Romeo and Juliet, but it would do.

He was also correct in assuming that Byrnes, one of nature's salesmen despite his mild manner, would turn the whole process of cleaning and restoration into a media event. The best restorers from the museums were called in to scrape away the paintwork of Mantini and remove the layer of protective varnish over the precious object underneath. Almost every week, bulletins on television would show the team of white-coated professionals—half scientific, half artistic—applying a variety of exotic solvents that could be relied upon to do their appointed task and no more. Then yet more programmes and articles in magazines monitored the second cleaning process, which would restore the painting to its original perfection.

Almost everybody knew by now that underneath the painting by Mantini there lay a portrait of Elisabetta di Laguna, the mistress of an earlier Marchese di Parma and, by repute, the most beautiful woman of her age. What someone like Raphael, who had made much less attractive women look like veritable Venuses, would have produced with such a sitter was anybody's guess. Critics from the *London Standard* to the *Baltimore Sun* speculated freely. Some even ventured to suggest that Leonardo's *Mona Lisa* would be knocked off its perch as the world's favourite painting.

While the picture was under wraps, the jockeying for position got under way amongst the likely buyers. The Louvre indicated its interest, if it could afford the price.

Two large New York banks and three pension funds in Tokyo also let it be known they might attend the auction. In an attempt to frighten off the opposition, the Getty Museum in Malibu Beach hinted that it might unleash all its vast buying-power to take possession. And all over the world, lesser millionaires and billionaires assessed their position, counted their money and attempted to work out whether they could, in a few years, sell it for a profit. Many decided they could.

When the picture was finally revealed to the public, the event was stage-managed in exquisite detail. The unveiling took place in a large meeting-room at the Savoy Hotel in the Strand, and hundreds of people were invited. The picture stood on a raised platform, covered with a large white sheet. Before the great moment, a presentation was made to the assembled press, television cameras, dignitaries from the worlds of museum and art-history faculties. The senior curator of the Louvre sat alongside the local staffer from Associated Press and the great Japanese collector Yagamoto; while the keeper of western art from the Dresdener Staatsgalerie was sandwiched between his great rival from one of the richest museums in the American Midwest and a sweaty individual from one of the London tabloids.

All of them had been served with champagne, courtesy of Byrnes Galleries, and all listened with appropriate attention as Byrnes himself ran through the now well-known story of how the painting was discovered; long forgotten in the little church in central Rome, and covered by another painting as a result of one of the greatest artistic fraud attempts of all time. Byrnes did a competent job of it, but was far from coming across as the archetype of the smooth art dealer. A small, timid-looking man with horn-rimmed spectacles and a bald head which ducked and bobbed nervously as he spoke, he was not at all like most people's image of an international aesthete.

Nor, to Flavia in the fifteenth row on the right, did he look like the Machiavellian beast of Jonathan Argyll's evidently fevered imagination. She was there largely out of curiosity; the presentation having come during one of her visits to London for informal discussions with the London art squad.

Flavia had gently asked her opposite number in London to organise an invitation. The squad was out in force to guard the picture, and Byrnes could hardly refuse them. So she sat and listened to him making his concluding remarks. Then he introduced Professor Julian Henderson, doyen of Renaissance studies, who gave a brief lecture. The picture, he told them, in an eminently polished delivery, was, without doubt, Raphael's masterpiece; the apogee of the Humanist ideal of feminine beauty.

The lecture hall was not one that the journalists in the audience were used to, but they listened politely, and the photographers got on with their business. Henderson concluded by comparing the picture to other portraits by Raphael, and suggesting that the evidence now indicated that Elisabetta had been the model for the portrait of Sappho in the mural of Parnassus in the Vatican. The new work that the discovery would engender was enough to keep historians of the Italian High Renaissance in business for years.

Amid minor laughter and light applause he sat down and Byrnes moved towards the picture.

Flavia was beginning to find the showbiz style of the meeting a little wearisome, and was glad that Byrnes avoided any excessive display in the final stages. Not that it was needed; the audience's sense of anticipation needed no further stimulation. With only a minor flourish, the cover was gently removed, and there was a quiet gasp as the onlookers, and the cameras, focused on what had become one of the most famous paintings in the world.

Because of the incessant coverage it had received in the last few months, almost everyone had some idea what the portrait looked like. Seeing it in the flesh was nonetheless exhilarating. It was a beautiful painting of a very beautiful woman. From her position, Flavia could not see very well, but it seemed to be a bust length with the head turned slightly to the right. Fair hair was gathered loosely at the back of the head so that the left ear was partly covered. The left hand reached up to touch a necklace, and the subject was dressed in a closefitting dress of a gorgeously rich red. The background was conventional, but excellently produced. The sitter—lean and with none of the fleshy appearance that made many of Raphael's Madonnas look just a little overweight—was in a room. In the left background was a window giving out to a wooded hill, on the right, wall hangings, a table and some ornaments. The organisation of the figure itself radiated an air of remarkable tranquillity, with just a hint of the sensuality that the painter so often brought out.

But she was most struck by the reaction from the audience. They were not admiring the delicacy of the brush strokes, the masterly application of shading or the subtleties of the composition, that was certain. They were ogling. Not a usual reaction for connoisseurs. She herself was caught up in the enthusiasm. The picture, both in its history and subject, was extraordinarily romantic. This most beautiful woman, nearly half a millenium old, had been lost for nearly three hundred years. It could hardly fail to capture the imagination. She even felt herself forgiving Byrnes.

THE enthusiasm that greeted Elisabetta's entry onto the world scene after her long absence carried the painting right through to the auction, held in the main sale room of Christie's about a month later. That affair also lived up to expectations.

The auctioneers knew how to put on a show. Expensively printed catalogues with full-colour photographs, a satellite link to sale rooms in Switzerland, New York and Tokyo, live television coverage in eight countries; these were the most obvious signs that an event of great importance was taking place. The atmosphere in the room, casually lined with other works of lesser significance, was electrifying. Like all good salesmen, the auctioneers had style. The sale was officially dubbed only "sixteenth- and seventeenth-century old master oils and drawings," and Elisabetta was humbly placed as number twenty-eight on the list. The only difference was that, unlike many of the other lots, the Raphael had not been given an estimated sale price.

The audience had risen to the occasion also. London auctions range widely in style, background and purpose. At one end, there are the routine sales held in the shabby auction rooms in insalubrious neighbourhoods like Marylebone where the main clientele are unshaven dealers who congregate to chat, eat sandwiches, and pick up paintings for a couple of hundred pounds.

At the very top of the pile are the great houses in St. James, where uniformed doormen open the broad brass doors, the employees speak with the accents of the privileged, and the clientele look as if they could buy a few hundred thousand pounds-worth of oil painting and not even notice. Even here, however, dealers tend to predominate, but these are the princes of their trade, with galleries in Bond Street or Fifth Avenue or the Rue de Rivoli. They are the sort of people who have enough to live on for a year if they sell one painting every three months, who own firms—not companies and never shops—that were often founded a century or more before. Not that this made them any more honest and less likely to break the law if necessary, but they generally did so more cautiously, more intelligently, and with greater decorum.

Like their clients, they knew how to behave appropriately. In the audience of maybe three hundred people, all but a dozen of the men wore their dinner jackets. The women, outnumbered around four to one, were dressed to match, with most in long ball gowns or wearing furs—until the heat of the camera lights made them intolerable. The air vibrated with the smell of a hundred mingling perfumes.

The sense of anticipation built up slowly as the lots were brought to the rostrum and the bidding started. A Maratta was sold for three hundred thousand pounds—the price instantly clicked up on the display board in four countries translated into dollars, Swiss francs and yen—and no one paid any attention. An Imperiali fetching a record price excited no interest whatsoever. Lot twenty-seven, a particularly fine old Palma oil-sketch which deserved greater consideration, was knocked down at an absurdly low price and bought.

Then came lot twenty-eight. The auctioneer, a man in his sixties who had seen it all before, knew well that the best way to generate excitement and loosen wallets was an utterly deadpan presentation. The slightest sign of enthusiasm or an apparent wish to manipulate the audience with a show of salesmanship would produce entirely the wrong effect. Understatement is always a virtue in such situations. As he spoke, two young men in brown overalls brought the picture and hung it on the easel to the right of the rostrum. It stood there, bathed in light—as one poetic television reporter put it afterwards—as if it were back on an altar as an object of worship itself.

"Lot twenty-eight. Raphael. A portrait of Elisabetta di

Laguna, about 1505. Oil on canvas, sixty-eight centimetres by a hundred and thirty-eight. I'm sure many of you know the background to this work, so we will start the bidding at twenty million pounds. What am I bid?"

To start the bidding at such a high price was audacious, but just the right touch of muted flamboyance needed. Only a few years ago to have *ended* the session on such a figure would have been a sensation. Only four pictures in the world had ever fetched more. Without any noise, and without any member of the audience appearing to move at all, the bidding flashed past thirty million, then thirty-five, then forty. At forty-two million, some dealers manning a rank of telephones along one side of the room spoke to their clients in dozens of different countries. At fifty-three million, some put down their phones and folded their arms, signifying that their clients had pulled out. At fifty-seven million it was clear that the bidding was down to two people, a burly man in the third row who insiders knew had acted in the past for the Getty Museum, and a small man who made his bids with a nervous gesture with his hand, chopping sideways briefly as though making a point in an animated conversation.

It was this second man who won. After he had offered sixty-three million pounds, the burly man with the purple cravat looked up, hesitated and then shook his head. There was silence for perhaps three seconds.

"Sold. For sixty-three million pounds. Yours, sir."

The room exploded in applause, the tension welling up suddenly then bursting into relief and euphoria. It was not only a record, but an enormous record. The only reservation in the minds of the professional part of the audience was who the buyer had been. The art world is a small universe and almost everyone in it knows everyone else and who they work for.

No one had the slightest idea who this man was, and he vanished through a side door before anybody could ask him.

4

IT took only a few days before the word seeped through the secret passages riddling the world of dealers, connoisseurs and collectors that the small unknown man who had outbid the Getty was a senior civil servant in the Italian treasury, sent to the sale with a blank cheque from the government and instructions to get the work at any cost. The news itself caused another mild stir. Like most other state museums, the Italian system was given an annual budget that was wholly inadequate. Like the curators of every museum in Europe, the director of the Museo Nazionale had had to stand by, consumed by a mixture of rage and envy, as work after precious work reached prices that his entire budget for the next twelve months could not have covered. But he was a man who regarded the saving of works for Italy as a moral duty, and had been lobbying everyone in authority for months to set aside more funds. He had won his point and, when Elisabetta came up for sale, had cajoled and fought for the government to honour its promises.

Clearly, some remarkable maneuvering had been going on in the labyrinthine and obscure network of intrigue known as the Italian government. In fact, it was another example of politics at work. The interest that the portrait had generated elsewhere in the world was nothing compared to that seen in Italy itself. The way that a cunning English dealer had snatched Elisabetta from the hands of State and Vatican, and had legally evaded all the restrictions designed to stop such an event, made the government appear foolish, the museum curators slow-witted, and the art historians incompetent.

And several members of the government remembered the furore that had preceded the founding of Bottando's sezione only a few years before. So the authorities gave way to the ferocious and persuasive lobbying, made available the special grant they had promised, and sent off their man. In some ways it was a daring thing to do: the opposition Communist Party instantly did its best to make capital out of the move by pointing to a dozen better ways of spending that sort of money. Others wrote polemical articles in the newspapers on the Italian budget deficit and how the country could not possibly afford such indulgences.

But the government, and particularly the arts minister,

had calculated correctly. He posed as a champion of the Italian heritage, willing to defend the patrimony at all costs. If Italy had lost such a valuable painting, then it must have it back. If this cost money, then so be it; that amount would be paid to safeguard the nation's artistic integrity. It turned out to be a popular move; opinion polls showed that the electorate's patriotic nerve had been touched. Besides, there is something peculiarly gratifying in owning the most expensive picture in the world, and to have outspent the Americans and Japanese in a fair fight. Outside the country also, the Italian move was applauded. Directors from national museums everywhere cited the purchase as an example for their own governments to follow; some newspapers even began pointing to the minister—a man of little administrative ability and small intelligence—as embodying the sort of dynamism and vision that could make an effective prime minister.

Which didn't endear him to the current incumbent, but as the government as a whole reaped some of the advantages of being considered effective, swift of foot and cultured—the last quality in some ways more important in Italy than the first two—nothing was said. But it was noted, and the minister was marked down for special attention in case he should show further signs of getting above himself.

The actual return of the painting was conducted like a state visit from a visiting sovereign. A month after the auction, once it had been put through a series of tests and examinations in London by specialists, it arrived in an air-force transport at Fiumicino airport and was carried in a procession—with attendant motorcycle outriders and armoured cars—to the National Museum. The armoured cars seemed a little excessive, but Bottando's department, in liaison with his comrades in the regular army, was taking no chances. The Brigate Rosse, the urban guerillas of the seventies, had lain dormant for several years, but you never knew.

In the Museo Nazionale itself, Elisabetta was set up like an icon. A room was emptied to take the portrait which would rest, behind the rope barrier keeping viewers ten feet away, in solitary splendour. Again, caution prevailed. Both police and curators remembered the sledgehammer attack on Michelangelo's *Pietà* in St. Peter's a few years before; too many pictures in recent years had been slashed with knives or peppered with pellets from shotguns by maniacs who claimed to be the archangel Gabriel, or resented the adulation of some long-dead artist while their own talents went unrecognised. And everyone agreed that the painting's fame made it a perfect target for some deranged attention-seeker.

Finally, the room was bathed in subdued lighting, with a single spotlight illuminating the work. The museum's interior designers freely admitted to their friends, if not to anybody else, that this was a bit melodramatic. Drawings, such as Leonardo's *Madonna* in the National Gallery in London, actually needed such protection from light to preserve them. Oil paintings were much more resilient and could do perfectly well in natural light. But the effect was splendid, creating an atmosphere of almost religious awe and causing visitors to speak in respectful, hushed tones which added greatly to the work's impact.

Visitors there were in abundance. In the first few months attendance at the museum doubled. A visit suddenly became almost compulsory not only for tourists—who had often left it out hitherto because of its inconvenient location out of the centre—but even for Romans themselves. Thousands of postcards were sold; Elisabetta di Laguna T-shirts were popular; a multi-national biscuit company paid the museum a fortune for the right to put her face on one of their products. Combined with the hugely increased entry fees, the museum directors calculated the state would have recovered most of the vast cost of the picture within four years if the painting's popularity continued at this rate.

FOR Bottando and his assistant, the return of the painting had triggered one of their busiest periods for years. Setting up security, keeping tabs on known national and international thieves, worrying lest anything should go wrong, chained them to their desks.

Bottando, looking at the work through the eyes of an old-time policeman whose budget was already not big enough, spent much of his time in a frenzy of anxiety. He knew perfectly well that, whatever the picture's artistic merits, it was a painted time bomb for his department. If anything should happen to it, the blame would move around the government with the speed of a ball in a pinball machine before coming to rest on his desk.

Much of his work, therefore, consisted of preparing his defences. Although not a cynical man, and no politician, he was no fool either. A lifetime's work under the aegis of the ministry of defence had taught him a great deal about survival techniques in a world that made fighting in the army seem genteel and civilised. So he spent many hours sweating over cautiously worded reports, drafted and redrafted memoranda and wasted a great deal of time taking a few, carefully selected, bureaucrats and politicians to dinner.

The result was not entirely to his liking, but better than nothing. He had lobbied for extra manpower, using Elisabetta as a way of making his case for a larger budget. In fact, the result was that the security staff of the Museo Nazionale was doubled. Although it was never stated directly, the effective conclusion was that his department was relieved of any responsibility for guarding the picture once it was hung.

This provided some protection. But Bottando realised, with a perception honed by years of watching for trouble, that there existed no official document proving his lack of responsibility, and that was worrying. Especially because in Cavaliere Marco Ottavio Mario di Bruno di Tommaso, the sublimely aristocratic director of the National Museum, he was dealing with a man who would have been a natural politician had he not gone into the museum business. A smoother operator, in fact, was not to be found in the Camera dei Deputati. Tommaso had had a painting snatched from under his very nose, had been forced to buy it back at an outrageous price, and had turned it into a triumph. Impressive, without a doubt.

He was reminded of the justice of this opinion as he stood talking to the director at a reception thrown to celebrate the picture's installation in the museum. A very select junket indeed. A sizeable chunk of the cabinet and their inevitable hangers-on; museum folk, the occasional academic, a few journalists just so the affair would reach the papers. Tommaso was, if anything, Bottando's superior in making sure glowing reports of his activities frequently adorned the pages of the newspapers.

"Taking a bit of a risk, aren't you? I mean, all these dubious types around your prized possession?" Bottando gestured contemptuously at the prime minister and an army chief peering at the work, cigarettes in hand.

Tommaso moaned softly in agreement. "I know. But it's difficult to ask the prime minister not to smoke. He gets withdrawal symptoms after ten minutes. We had to switch off all the fire alarms to make sure they weren't all drenched by the sprinklers. Can't say it makes me all that happy. But, there you are. What can you do? These people will insist on sharing the limelight." He shrugged.

The conversation dragged on for a few minutes more, and then Tommaso slid off to talk to others. He was always like that. Everybody got the regulation five minutes of urbane conversation. He was a perfect host; Bottando merely wished that he didn't make you feel it all the time.

He was always pleasant, always remembered everyone's name, always recalled something about your last conversation with him to make you think he valued your company. Bottando hated him. The more so because he'd just sprung a very nasty surprise.

There was to be another liaison committee, he'd said. Were there not enough already, for heaven's sake? A joint meeting of the museum and the police, to discuss security matters in the museum: Bottando heading the police end and Antonio Ferraro, the head of sculpture, the museum side. It had been Ferraro's idea, apparently. Serve him right. Had Bottando heard about this in advance, he could have sabotaged the whole thing. But Tommaso had gone ahead, getting all the various approvals, before broaching the subject.

It was, of course, true that what this place did need was a long, hard look at its security procedures, which were neolithic. But a committee wasn't going to achieve much and, in fact, it wasn't intended to. Instead, Tommaso meant it to serve as a layer of protection between him and responsibility if anything should go wrong.

The only person Bottando felt sorry for was Ferraro, standing over on the other side of the room. Tall, broad, and powerful-looking. Dark hair, of the sort that clung to his scalp as though it had been heavily annointed with hair dressing. A voluble conversationalist, one of those who tends to interrupt you in mid-sentence so that he can continue his enthusiastic narrations. Mid-thirties, with a permanent look of mild sarcasm on his face. A clever, impatient man. No wonder he and Tommaso never got on well; neither was prepared to accept the other in anything but a subservient role. Maybe Bottando could have him replaced on the committee with someone a bit more amenable?

"You're scowling," said a voice by his side. "I deduce that you've just been talking to our beloved chief."

Bottando turned around, and smiled. Enrico Spello was unofficially the deputy director and someone he had a certain liking for. "Right as usual. How did you guess?"

Spello clasped his hands together to indicate the mysteries of human intuition. "Simple. I always look like that after a conversation with Tommaso as well."

"But he's your boss. You've a right to dislike him. He's always pleasant to me."

"Of course. He's always delightful to me, as well. Even when he's cutting my budget by twenty-five per cent."

"He's done that? When?"

"Oh, it's been going on for a year or more. No interest in the Etruscans any more. For archaeologists and antiquarians. What's needed is more brightness, stuff to bring in the crowds. As you know, he's a bit of a whizz kid, our Tommaso. My department gets sliced so he can afford some very expensive beige fabric on the walls of western art."

"Is yours the only department to be cut?" Bottando asked.

"Oh, no. But it's one of the worst. It has lost our friend over there a lot of popularity." He smiled whimsically.

Bottando felt for the man. He was a real scholar, the sort of person who was dying out in the museum world. He lived, breathed and slept Etruscan antiquities. No one knew more about those mysterious people than Spello. His sort were now being replaced by administrators, by fund raisers and by entrepreneurs. Not at all like the short, stout and eccentrically dressed Spello.

"I didn't know he had any popularity to lose," Bottando commented.

"He didn't really. I don't know why he bothers. He's got so much money he doesn't have to."

Bottando raised an eyebrow. "Indeed? I never knew that."

Spello looked sideways at him. "And you call yourself a policeman? I thought you were meant to know everything. Vast family riches, so I'm told. Won't do him any good. One day he'll be found in his office with a knife in his back. Then you'll be spoiled for suspects."

"Where should I start?"

"Well," Spello began, considering the matter. "I trust you would do me the honour of making me top suspect. Then there's the people in Non-Italian Baroque, who've been shunted into a tiny little attic where no one can ever find them. Impressionism doesn't at all like his decision to merge them with Realism, and Glassware greatly resents the imperialistic designs of Silver. Quite a hornet's nest, in fact. Our little dining-room resounds daily to tales of his outrages, past and present."

"And which past ones do you have in mind at the moment?" Bottando prompted. He loved gossip, and realised Spello wanted to tell him some anecdote. Besides, he was irritated that he hadn't known of the Tommaso money.

"Ah. I was thinking of the Case of the Bum Correggio. This was back in the sixties, when our friend was keeper of pictures at Treviso. Nice museum, traditional starting place for One Who is Destined to Rise in the World. Being an ambitious and aggressive young man, Tommaso began to buy pictures from abroad, commandeering almost everyone else's budget to do so.

"He bought dozens of pictures and established his reputation as a thrusting up-and-comer. He likes buying pictures, you may have noticed. He alienated everyone else in the museum by doing so but, what the hell? He'd soon be moving on to better things.

"But he made a false step. He bought a Correggio for a considerable amount of money, and hung it in the gallery. Then the whispers started. An article appeared, saying that on stylistic grounds it might not be genuine. Then some pieces of provenance were dredged up suggesting it was merely a copy. He forces the dealer—none other than Edward Byrnes—to take it back. But the storm over his competence continues, nonetheless.

"This is where our friend's genius comes in. His friends in Rome whisper into ears. He bludgeons his director—a sweet and naïve man—into taking the fire. The director resigns, and Tommaso, enhancing his reputation, resigns out of loyalty. He goes out into the wilderness for a brief period but is soon back, climbing the ladder to the stars. And there he is, in his firmament.

"So you see," Spello added, looking around him at the now thinning room, "we may seem a happy family, but what a maelstrom of discontent is there. One mistake from our friend over there, and there'll be a queue, half a kilometre long, waiting to tear his throat out."

5

DESPITE the concern that the presence of Elisabetta continued to create, the work of the department had to go on as much as possible. If the public was entranced by the picture, the art thieves paused only momentarily before getting back to their proper business.

In fact, the furore might have encouraged more activity; with contemplation on the value and transportability of a small piece of canvas tempting more people to try their luck on other, less illustrious objects. This was tiresome, but in some ways satisfying, as the department's success rate improved by picking up the amateurs. Removing an Italian statue or picture is often very simple, merely a question of breaking down an often frail door, loading the work into a car and driving off. Any second-rate crook can manage it. Getting rid of it afterwards, however, is a different matter. You can't just take a hot painting in to a sale room and sell it, and if you want to pass it on to a dealer you have to know the honest ones from the dishonest ones. Successfully stealing works of art is a highly skilled occupation which, unlike many others, continues to breed practitioners of great ability.

It was because of the quiet but persistent activity of a master craftsman that several months after the arrival of Elisabetta in state to Rome, and once much of the excitement had died away to little more than an expanded inflow of income to the Museo Nazionale's coffers, Flavia returned once more to London.

It was for yet another liaison meeting, a gathering of policemen from France, Italy, Greece and Britain, all brought together because of one man, thought to be French and suspected of running a thriving business in the theft of Greek icons.

Icons are relatively little known outside the art world, an obscure area that interests only the enthusiast. The pictures, generally on wooden panels and hung in Orthodox churches to assist the focusing of attention during prayer, are often difficult to appreciate. With simple backgrounds of gold, their stylised appearance is an acquired taste, especially as the absence of perspective makes them difficult for viewers brought up on the dynamism of the Renaissance. But once the taste is formed, they can become a passion, the stark elegance and uncluttered forms giving an aura of peacefulness and tranquillity which the more robust, active pieces produced in the West rarely approach.

More importantly, perhaps, they command high prices and the market for them is notably more crooked than for other types of art. Because one of the major sources is the Soviet Union, smuggling them is commonplace. Russian icons are also regularly brought out by *émigrés* who are forbidden to take out currency. They are smuggled to Vienna and on to Tel Aviv, then sent on to the market via New York and London. Buying them is cast almost as a blow for freedom, and few dealers or collectors worry themselves about their origin.

All these factors help create a market which Jean-Luc Morneau evidently found attractive—assuming that the deductions of the Sûrété were correct and that it was this Paris-based dealer who was behind the thefts. When the monastery on the island of Amorgos in the Cyclades contacted the local policeman, who in turn passed a message to Athens, which in due course made enquiries around Europe, Morneau's name kept on appearing, although no hard evidence could be produced to warrant any sort of action.

Whoever it was, the technique used was simple. A tourist appears on the doorstep of the monastery asking to see the church. Once inside, he takes photographs, and particularly snaps away at the icon above the altar. He then thanks the monk at the gate, makes a donation and departs.

He returns many months later, sporting a beard, moustache or dark glasses to make recognition unlikely. He is again left to wander as he pleases. He checks to see the church is empty, goes up to the altar and unzips the large camera case. He takes out the copy he has painted from the photographs, swaps it for the genuine one over the altar and puts this carefully into his bag. He leaves the island on the next boat—the visit is timed so that the boat leaves only an hour or so afterwards—heads for Crete or Rhodes where airport customs are scarce, and flies out of the country.

The copy left behind on Amorgos, and on about twenty other islands, as well as a few sites in the north-east of Italy, is detected as a fake the moment that experts examine it. But it is very competent and quite able to withstand the normal scrutiny it receives, half-hidden in the semi-twilight of the church, from both monks and the occasional sightseer. According to the best recollection of the monks, it had done so for more than a year. Other monasteries had been admiring their copies for even longer.

The finger pointed to Morneau firstly because he was a dealer in icons, secondly because he had been trained as a painter, and thirdly because he was not known for his honesty. But, there the evidence had dried up, and the meeting had been called so that efforts could be directed towards tracking down some of the paintings by discreet enquiries.

The Greek police also wanted help in the search for Morneau, who had vanished from sight. French checks had established that he had vacated his studio in the Place des Abbesses some time ago. Without knowing where he was, it was that much more difficult to establish where he had been. Certainly the evidence of the monasteries was of little help; one reported the visitor with the camera case as French, others as Swedish, German, American and Italian. They had all failed to identify him from photographs.

The meeting to discuss the matter was largely inconclusive, mainly because one young and none-too-serious Englishman had sighed and ventured that he wished he could have thought of a crime like that. The remark irritated the Greeks, who had responded by making remarks about crooked French dealers, which sent the Gallic contingent into a sulk. The encounter, indeed, was no great symbol of European cooperation.

It was also as an indirect result of this somewhat inconclusive meeting that Flavia met Jonathan Argyll once more. He had written to her several months before, asking to see her if she should come to England, and saying that he wouldn't mind returning the favour and taking her to dinner. She had not written back, partly because there had been no immediate plan to go to England, and partly because she hated writing letters; which, to her mind, made up a pretty good reason.

But evenings alone in big cities can be very dull, especially when the days are short, the weather is cold and the rain, as always in London, is coming down in a light, but persistent drizzle. It was impossible to walk around either to see sights or to window-shop. Going to restaurants on your own has little attraction, the cinemas weren't showing anything that interested her, the one play she wanted to see was booked solid and the thought of a lonely evening in a hotel room with an improving book made those little twinges of imminent depression noticeable.

So, having exhausted all other possibilities, she picked up the phone and gave him a ring. He was instantly delighted to hear her, and invited her to go and eat immediately. She accepted, and he suggested she come round to his flat. This she considered, assessed for possible trouble, and refused. Even Englishmen could act funny when in their own apartments and, while she had no doubts about her ability to deal with any awkward situation, it always ruined an evening.

"Oh go on. I'm not sure which restaurant to go to and it would be much easier if you came here first. It's not very far from the tube."

A sort of uncalculating friendliness in his request made her change her mind. She agreed to meet him at his flat at seven-thirty, was given directions, and put down the phone.

GETTING to Notting Hill Gate from her hotel was easy. On the whole, Flavia's main objection to London was simply the size of the place and the inhuman way it was laid out. In Rome, she lived about fifteen minutes' walk away from the office, in a quiet and inexpensive part of town near Augustus's mausoleum that had an abundance of restaurants, innumerable shops and a boisterous population. But London was entirely different. Almost no one seemed to live anywhere near the centre and everyone spent hours every day on the tubes or trains either going to work or going home again. And the neighbourhoods they lived in were generally unutterably dull, with few shops and an atmosphere of respectability that made you think they were all tucked up in bed by nine-thirty with a glass of hot milk. The constant cavalcade of streetlife, of people wandering around for the sake of it, greeting their friends, having a drink, everything that made city life worthwhile, scarcely existed. London was not Flavia's idea of a good time.

Argyll's part of Notting Hill lay beyond the respectable bit that surrounded the tube station, in the less opulent regions beyond. The building was neither among the best nor the worst that the area had to offer. He lived on the top floor of a terraced house halfway along the street and, when she rang the doorbell, bellowed into a faulty, crackling ansaphone that she should keep walking up the stairs until she ran out.

His flat showed distinct signs of a very hurried and only partly successful attempt at flight. Mounds of notes lay in boxes; open suitcases, half filled with clothes and books, were on the floor; a pile of miscellaneous socks nestled up against the bottle of white wine that Argyll had evidently just been out to buy in her honour.

"Moving, are you?" she observed, noting that this was

not the sort of conclusion that required the brains of a Sherlock Holmes to reach.

"Yup," he replied, uncorking the bottle and peering into it to see how much cork was left floating in the wine. He frowned in disapproval at the debris, then looked up with a happy smile. "Farewell London, hello again Rome. For about a year, maybe more. Until I finish the damn thesis. I've done all the English end, so everything I need is in Italy. Which is pretty convenient, if you ask me."

"I thought you were impoverished."

"So I was. However, not at the moment. It's one of the unforeseen spin-offs of that Raphael."

"How so?"

"Well, you see, I was invited to a party, and there was Edward Byrnes. He sort of sidled up to me in a sheepish fashion and we got talking. The upshot of it was that he as near as dammit apologised for pinching the picture. Not, of course, that he admitted any double-dealing. Independent research leading in the same direction, and so on. Not his picture, anyway, you know. Entire coincidence, the whole thing. That's as may be. I don't believe it. He got wind of it through me, somehow. The important thing was, he offered a disguised form of compensation. His firm has a scholarship for art historians, and basically he said that if I applied for it, I'd probably be given it. So I did, and so I was."

"And you took it?"

Argyll paused for a moment. "Well, I thought, why the hell not? The picture's out of my reach for ever, Byrnes has a lot of money thanks to me. I could have stood on my dignity and refused to touch his filthy money, how dare you insult me, sir. But he'd still be as rich, and I'd still be as poor. By rights, I suppose, he should have offered me a couple of million. But he didn't, and it was this or nothing."

"What did he mean, not his picture?"

"Just that, apparently. That's the story he's evidently putting around, probably because of jealousy in the trade. He was acting on commission. Someone else got him to buy it and so someone else now has the money, presumably."

"Who?" asked Flavia, intrigued.

"Didn't say. I didn't ask, to tell you the truth, because it's such obvious nonsense. Besides, I was too busy fantasising about going back to Italy."

"You'd never make a very good policeman," she observed.

"I know. But I don't plan to. It struck me as such a silly story, I dismissed it instantly. I mean to say, can you see any self-respecting dealer having a Raphael on his hands and tamely letting it go?" He paused for a moment while he fished for bits of cork with his finger, dredging them out a fragment at a time.

"Disgusting of me. Sorry about that," he said apologetically.

He poured, she sipped, he sat on the floor and they talked inconsequentially about her trip, his research, how he found his flat. They spoke in Italian and about Italy, and Argyll grew gently and fondly enthusiastic. He loved it in the way that only the repressed, monochromatic inhabitants of cold northern countries can fall for the colourful exuberance of the Mediterranean. But his was no goggle-eyed, blind devotion; he knew the country well, warts and all. The inefficiencies, rigidities, narrow-mindedness of Italy he understood and accepted. He also knew its art, and could talk with nostalgic delight of the long and weary trips he had made by bus and by foot to the more obscure delights that Italy likes to secrete in inaccessible places. It occurred to Flavia that he might get on well with Bottando. Then he changed the subject back and they talked about London, work and museums. He held up a finger as he poured her another glass of wine. "There was, by the way, another reason for taking Byrnes's money. It struck me as a sort of victory."

She looked at him, puzzled, "Some victory," she said.

"Wait and see," he replied, kneeling down by a large cardboard box and rummaging through dozens of bits of paper. "Now, where did I put it? That's the trouble when you pack. You always need the things at the bottom of the boxes. Ah. Here it is. I must show you. I think you'll find it funny."

ARGYLL explained that on his return to England, after the débâcle in the carabinieri cells, he had thrown himself back into the subject of Mantini with vigour. His motives were not any great love of art history, nor any particular devotion to resurrecting the reputation of his chosen painter—a man who by any stretch of the imagination was fairly second-rate. Rather, it had become a matter of pride that, having spent a few years on the subject, he was going to get something to show for it all, even if it was just a piece of paper and the right to be called Doctor Argyll.

He went on to say how he had made a resolute attempt to forget about Raphael and associated subjects. His painter had been fairly popular among English tourists in Rome in the early eighteenth-century, and many of them had commissioned some minor work from him as a memento of their stay; the eighteenth-century equivalent of buying a postcard of the Spanish Steps. Generally speaking, he turned out somewhat derivative landscapes in the style of Claude Lorrain or Gaspard Dughet which were held in high esteem at the time. As he was compiling a *catalogue raisonné* of the artist's work, he had written to almost every country-house owner in England to ask whether they had any. He had also gone to visit several houses, to look through their archives for any evidence of when the works were bought, how they were acquired and at what price.

On one of these ventures he had ended up in Backlin House in Gloucestershire, a vast, chilly pile still lived in by the original family even though they could clearly no longer afford it. Had they been sensible, he said, they would have given the place away to the National Trust and gone to live in the South of France, like the Clomortons had done after the war.

The muniments room, where the family papers were kept in dusty, mouldy obscurity, had made the rest of the house seem positively jolly. One look had almost persuaded him to go straight back home.

"A man from the Historic Manuscripts Commission came round in 1903 to catalogue the papers but died of influenza halfway through. I'm not surprised. If I hadn't taken the precaution of bringing a pair of mittens, a woolly hat and a hip flask I might well have gone under myself. The experienced researcher is prepared for all eventualities," he added loftily.

Because of the poor gentleman's untimely demise, the papers had never been sorted and a catalogue never published. And because of that, no one had been near them for years. So Argyll, when he finally made his way into the attic that contained four hundred years of miscellaneous memories, found a huge number of dust-covered rolls of documents, chests of estate vouchers, bundle upon bundle of legal materials, and a whole series of nineteenth-century cardboard boxes labelled "first earl," "second earl" and so on.

On the whole, the thousands of papers were arranged randomly, or if there were any order, he failed to grasp what it was. However, a few boxes bore the traces of the old archivist, and had evidently been arranged for examination before he died. These were given rough labels. One large box was titled "eighteenth-century letters."

"This was my great discovery," Argyll said. "One sheath was entirely of letters to the owner of the house, Sir Robert Delmé, from his sister Arabella."

"So?" asked Flavia, her manners beginning to fight a battle for dominance over her impatience.

"Arabella was a great lady, the sort that died out when the eighteenth century was through. She had four husbands in all, and outlived the lot. She was about to take on number five when she herself keeled over from excess cognac at the age of eighty-seven. The point is that husband number two was none other than our friend the Earl of Clomorton—that noted connoisseur of Raphael—and ten of the letters dated from this period."

Argyll explained that most of the letters were of little interest—London gossip, details of the doings of the Prince of Wales, as well as scabrous comments about the innumerable inadequacies of her husband. Although wealthy, the second Earl clearly did not rate highly with his wife, was parsimonious to a fault and seemed greatly lacking in judgement.

"He was exactly the sort of person the average Roman art dealer could see coming a mile off. It would have been a point of honour amongst them to foist rubbish onto him at vast expense. All he really cared about deeply were his haemorrhoids, if Lady A is to be believed. He seems to have kept up a non-stop monologue on the subject for years on end. Painful, no doubt, but they ruin the atmosphere at breakfast."

Two of the letters came from the period in which the

earl died, one immediately before, the second afterwards. "Here," said Argyll, shuffling through a set of papers in a manila folder, "I copied them down. Have a look."

Flavia picked up the first sheet of paper and squinted at it to decipher Argyll's rapid and untidy scrawl. *Dearest Brother*, it began, *As I've no doubt you are acquainted from the* Gazette, *my Lord has returned to these shores from his travels. My! how he is changed! No more the ruddy sportsman; the soft airs of Italy have turned him into a true connoisseur of the arts! I cannot tell you how much his new occupation causes me mirth. He parades all day in his finest French lace, giving the servants orders in what he considers fine Italian. They do not understand him so do as they please, as usual. Worst of all, his fascinations have unclenched his fist. It appears he has been attempting to buy up all of Italy, and plunge his family into ruin in the process. Some of his baubles have already been brought to the house; I intend to hang them only in the darkest corners, so visitors will not easily discern how my husband has been impos'd upon by these foreign sellers. He promised me pictures by the finest Italian hands; he has brought me the merest daubs, the grossest of impositions. Only in price do his prizes rank with the fairest productions of the masters. The final blow is yet to fall, however; he has been in London with Mr. Paris for the past three weeks fussing over one final consignment of ruins by those wretches of Roman scene-painters who delighted in taking his money. My Lord tells me—in his most mysterious voice—these will delight and amaze me beyond comparison. I confess, I do not see how I could be more amazed. It seems that he spent more than seven hundred pounds for one of these, which surely will turn out to be worth not more than half-a-crown.*

The letter then continued with local gossip and politics, complaints about servants and news about the death of some obscure relation's daughter. Then it got back to her husband, and the writer's venom began to be given free rein: *I have told you many times in the past, dear brother,* she continued, *about my Lord's amorous adventures. But less so of late after I threw that scene over the miserable hussy he was disgracing himself with before he left for his tour. I confess, when I told him then that I would cut his throat should he ever humiliate me thus again, the colour drained straight out of his cheeks! My dear brother, I was so convincing even I believed I would indeed do so. But the threat restored him to the way of fidelity. A scrub is ever thus, however. He seems still determined to humiliate our family name. My Lord arrives from London in two days' time. I leave you to think of the welcome he will receive from, your most affectionate sister, Arabella.*

"There," said Argyll, triumphantly. "What do you think of that, eh?"

Flavia shrugged. "So he was a dirty old sod. What should I think of it?"

"Weren't paying attention, were you? Look again. 'Wretched scene painter'—Mantini. 'Air of mystery,' that fits it well. 'Seven hundred pounds'—a vast price to pay for a picture then."

"So she's talking about the imminent arrival of Elisabetta. What of it?"

"But look at what she says. She says it is a painting of ruins—no doubt in a classical landscape—that is coming."

"So?"

"The painting of Elisabetta was found under a Repose on the Flight to Egypt. Odd, eh?" He leaned back in triumph after delivering a statement he evidently considered stunning.

"Well, frankly, no. It isn't," said an unimpressed Flavia. "Maybe she was referring to the quality of the picture, not its subject. Besides, we all know it was the wrong one."

Argyll had the look of someone who had been expecting dutiful admiration rather than counter-arguments. "Oh. Didn't think of that," he said.

"But," he said with renewed enthusiasm, lighting another of Flavia's cigarettes and tossing the match into his empty wineglass. "Listen. The common link here is the dealer, Sam Paris. He watched Mantini at work in Rome, and he saw the picture unpacked in London. If a different one had arrived on the boat, he would have noticed. But he evidently didn't, as Clomorton was still under the impression that everything was going to plan."

Flavia nodded thoughtfully, but without conviction. "Well, I'll give you that much."

"And it seems that no one noticed anything wrong until the painting was cleaned. Therefore Mantini must have painted a picture of ruins over the Raphael. Still OK?"

Flavia pursed her lips. "Well, maybe. But maybe Paris was in it as well, and agreed to send off a different picture. He was an art dealer after all, and if I remember rightly he disappeared afterwards. To any self-respecting policeman that would count as suspicious behaviour. And there is an internationally acclaimed Raphael hanging in the Museo Nazionale, which doesn't do your argument any good at all. Although I must confess I'm still not sure what your argument *is*."

"I don't really have one, yet. I don't suppose it's important. But it will make a nice footnote. Wouldn't it be splendid if they'd got the wrong Raphael? The very thought has kept me in good humour for weeks."

THE idea had fully restored Argyll's good spirits, and he walked along the wet, shiny pavements with a light step, skipping nimbly out of the way of the showers of water thrown up by buses and cars plunging through the deep puddles caused by blocked-up drains. He opened a vast black umbrella, the sort used by professional walkers in the rain, and stuck his elbow out.

Almost without thinking, Flavia rested her hand gently on the proferred arm. She couldn't remember that anyone had ever done such a quaint thing to her before. Furtive arms sliding round the waist before moving northwards, yes, in abundance; a cold and deliberate distance from her, which had been her last boyfriend's way of communicating displeasure, she was used to. But this had a quiet gentleness about it, giving her the opportunity delicately not to notice and shun the offer if she chose. Extraordinarily old-fashioned. But practical, and sweetly charming; it kept them close enough together so that both could keep dry under the awning of the huge umbrella.

"I thought we could go to a Thai restaurant," he said. "Roman food is very good, but when I was there I found myself craving something with spice in."

Flavia made no reply, and barely even heard him as he kept up a steady flow of chatter on inconsequential subjects. At the restaurant, she nodded absentmindedly as he asked if she wanted anything to drink, and nodded again when he suggested trying some sake, which she had never heard of. Then she applied herself to reading the menu.

"Why do you think it would be nice if the picture was the wrong one? I think it would be dreadful—the department is paying for this, by the way," she said, once the waiter had taken the order, delivered a bottle in a vase of hot water, and vanished. It occurred to her that it was the first time she had asked him a question and been properly interested in the reply. His newfound buoyancy had transformed his character into something much more agreeable, although he showed signs of tipping over the edge into smugness. He was, certainly, not quite as dimwitted as he seemed.

"Certainly not. You paid last time. Besides, this is meant to be a sort of apology for boring you to death in Rome. And don't worry, this is on Sir Edward Byrnes. I got my first cheque yesterday. As for the Raphael, just think of the number of respected authorities who are at this very moment battling with each other to get out their books on the New Raphael first. Think how many have made a fortune writing adulatory articles in magazines and newspapers. Better still, think what wallies they'd look if it was revealed that they had been heaping admiring adjectives upon a dud. You married?"

"No, I'm not." She paused and downed the small glass of sake. It tasted of almost nothing, but was warm. She filled her glass again and drank that too. The heat made up somewhat for its evident lack of alcohol. "Have you told anyone about this?"

"Not a soul. I learnt my lesson last time."

"Listen. Restrain yourself and be sensible. I know the whole business upset you, but the Raphael can't be a dud. Every art historian in the world has written an article about it. Every single one of them agrees that it's genuine. I know they make mistakes; but they can't all be wrong. You can't set up an inconclusive fragment by a woman concentrating mainly on her husband's sexual peccadilloes against the agreed opinion of the most distinguished art connoisseurs alive."

"I don't see why not. As you say, people make mistakes, sometimes whoppers. A sizeable chunk of art history consists of unravelling other people's errors and substituting your own. All the art galleries in the world are full of things labelled 'after Velazquez' or 'circle of Titian' which were drooled over for years as fine works from the master's hand. Boyfriend?"

Flavia refilled her glass. "No. But how do you prove it?" she asked. "If everyone has committed themselves to calling it a Raphael, it would be difficult to persuade them to change their minds. It's all a matter of opinion. If enough people say it's genuine, then it is. Besides, I think you're playing games. You don't really think it's a dud at all, do you?"

"Not really," he said sadly, ladling out the rice and experimenting with his chopsticks. "Wishful thinking, I suppose. I was enjoying fantasising about finding some conclusive fragment. Think of the embarrassment. 'New light on Raphael's Elisabetta.' Short, pithy little article. Bang. Art historians doing the decent thing and jumping out of windows or locking themselves in rooms with loaded pistols. Turmoil in the museum. Red faces in the government. All that taxpayers' money down the drain. I can almost see the editorials now. Attachment? Cat?"

He evidently found his train of thought quite delightful. He spooned some more food, and poured some more sake.

"No. What's that got to do with it?"

"Nothing. It's just that I like cats."

They ate in silence, which Flavia eventually broke. "At least I had better tell the General when I get back," she said, sipping meditatively. Extraordinary. The whole bottle was empty already. "Then he can do with it whatever he wants. Wastepaper bin most likely. But if anything does happen, then at least he won't be able to complain that he wasn't warned. I am single, unattached, and intend to stay that way. Men," she continued, wondering both why she was saying this and why her head was buzzing slightly, "are frightened of me. I dislike them. Generally speaking," she added cautiously, squinting at him. "So we are all happy. I feel sick."

In fact, she was extremely drunk, and remembered thinking very clearly to herself, before such an effort became too difficult, that she would resent her host a great deal when she recovered for not having told her that sake was a good deal stronger than wine, and much more vicious in its effects. "My last boyfriend used to tell me . . ." she began mournfully, but forgot what it was halfway through. It hadn't been nice though. He'd been very angry when she'd finally walked out. Thought that was his job. Accused her of being unfaithful. Silly sod. No, that was Clomorton. Not her. It was too much effort. She was probably fast asleep even before Argyll arranged her on his sofa. Must have been asleep, in fact. At least, she hadn't protested when he dropped her on the stairs.

FLAVIA woke in a panic and with a wicked head. She was booked on an Alitalia flight for Rome—all Italian civil servants travel on the national airline as a way of circulating revenue from department to department—which was due to leave at eleven-thirty. Argyll was nowhere around, but a note on the table read, "Had to go out. If I'm not back when you wake, coffee in kitchen. Hope your head is OK. You're a great drunk."

She had no time for coffee, despite the fact that she

would clearly die without it. She had no time to dress either, so it was just as well she had been deposited on the sofa fully clothed. She reckoned she had about two hours to get back to the hotel, pack, check out and make her way to Heathrow: department accountants always frown on additional costs caused by missing planes.

The head and the hurry put all thoughts of art out of her mind. Instead, she behaved more like a dogged automaton, the determination not to miss her flight constituting the only flicker of mental activity in an otherwise inoperative brain. She forgot all about Argyll, sake, Thai food and Raphael.

Flavia made the plane, ran down to the toilets the moment the seatbelt sign flickered off, and did her best to restore herself to human appearance. For the rest of the flight she persecuted the stewardesses unmercifully, demanding cup after cup of thick, strong coffee, aspirins and glasses of orange juice. She had to pay for the orange juice herself, accountants also frowning on self-indulgence, and it wasn't even much good. But it had some positive effects, and she was recovered enough by the time she arrived back home—grateful, above all, that it was Friday—to check through her accumulated mail before stepping into the bath.

A quiet and relaxing weekend allowed her to recover fully from the effects of oriental brewing. She occupied herself by being utterly domesticated in a way unusual for her—tidying the flat, doing some shopping, taking some clothes to the dry-cleaners. She forgot about work almost entirely until she made the brief walk to the office at eight-thirty the following Monday.

Paolo, the colleague whom she liked the most, greeted her. She asked what had been going on since she left.

"One case of jewellery, two and a half thousand eighteenth-century books, four paintings, thirty-eight prints. All gone. And the usual threats against that Raphael; somebody or other decided *we* should deal with them. We've had about a hundred sent over from the museum—part of the General's new committee work. Poor man, it's driving him to drink . . ."

They were settling down for a good and relaxing early morning conversation when Bottando stuck his head round the door. "Ah, there you are, my dear. Good trip? Splendid. Come up to my office and tell me about it in five minutes, would you?"

He vanished again. Paolo looked at the door. "He seems very edgy these days. I think he's still worrying about how to avoid landing in it if anything goes wrong with that damn painting. Don't know why. In the last few weeks he's surrounded this department with more defences and bureaucratic outworks than Fort Knox."

Flavia shrugged. "Maybe. Still, that reminds me of something I wanted to tell him. It might make him relax a bit."

She went up the stairs, walked through his door without knocking, as usual, and sat herself on his armchair. She summarised the meeting swiftly, then briefly ran over Argyll's tale about his researches.

"I thought I'd better tell you," she ended lamely. Bottando had his Silly-Little-Woman look on his face. He rarely used it, especially on her. "What do you think should be done about it?" she said.

"Nothing. File it and forget it. Better still, don't even file it. I'm much too old to go looking for trouble, and the very thought of telling the curator of the National Museum that he might have an old copy on his hands makes my pension start to shrink before my very eyes."

"But we should do something, surely? A quiet warning, a little suggestion?"

"My dear, if you didn't have me to protect you you'd be eaten alive. Now be sensible and think. The minister of defence is a Socialist, correct? And the arts minister is a Christian Democrat. And they don't like each other. Now, an old southern Socialist under this Socialist defence minister lets out the word that the arts minister has goofed in a big way. Do they say 'thank you for the warning, good of you to tell us?' Not likely. They suspect a conspiracy by the minority parties in the government to nobble their newly rising star and bring the DCI into disrepute. But they look anyway, discover the picture is genuine, and one ageing general, looking forward to his retirement, is wheeled out on to the scaffold to restore peace and harmony in the coalition. Preceded, I might add, by his very best assistant who is a notorious member of the Communist Party . . ."

"No I'm not. Membership's lapsed."

"Ex-member," her boss amended, "who is exactly the

sort of person who would come up with a naïve plot to undermine the government."

"But what if it really isn't genuine?"

"If it isn't, they have a scandal on their hands. But we keep out of it, stand on the sidelines and watch. Our job is to protect that painting, not to run around causing trouble. And whatever evidence we produce will have to be very, very persuasive. You remember that Watteau that caused all the fuss a few years ago?"

Flavia nodded.

"Pronounced as genuine by everyone, and sold to the States for a fortune. And what happens? Someone writes an article saying it's a fake. Says that if you look in the background you can see the word 'Merde' written clear as day. I've seen it myself, he is quite right. The painting popped up from nowhere, it has no history, no one has ever mentioned it before. It's ninety-five per cent certain it's a phoney. But who admits it? Not the museum, which paid three million dollars, not the art dealer who might have to give the money back, and not the critics and historians, who have already said how wonderful it is. So there it stays, despite clear and conclusive evidence that it's a monstrous hoax.

"Now you come to our Raphael, which cost twenty-five times as much, and has a history that can be traced back to the artist's brush. If it was a phoney the head of the National Museum would have to resign, and his patron, the minister, would have to go too, because he appropriated this purchase as his idea." He walked over to the window and stared out of it onto the façade of San Ignazio opposite.

"And he would have to be replaced, and the Socialists, the Liberals, the Republicans and all of them would demand that they be given his ministry because he had made such a mess. And the Christian Democrats would refuse because even now they only have a majority of one in the cabinet. And the government would duly collapse once more." He waved an arm in the direction of the Chamber of Deputies, up next to the ice-cream store where Flavia had taken Argyll.

"Can you imagine how much every museum head, politician, academic and newspaper critic would be mobilised to assert that, without any doubt, the picture was genuine? The proof that it was not would have to be three hundred per cent certain, absolutely unassailable and without the slightest glimmering of doubt.

"And what you and this man Argyll have got isn't. Any academic worth his salt would make mincemeat of it.

"I don't mind taking some risks," he added, sitting down again and staring at her firmly. "But I am damned if I am going to commit suicide for a hunch concocted by a walking disaster like that man Argyll. They would eat him for breakfast—that is if they took any notice of him at all—disappointed and impoverished scholar, nursing a grudge, tries to get his revenge by starting a slanderous rumour. They'd wipe him out. They might even be right."

6

"DEAR me, what a day," sighed Bottando, reaching out and tapping the waiter on the arm as he passed. "Another?"

Spello shook his head. "No, thank you. I find alcohol a very poor consolation for an afternoon like this. A coffee, however, would be welcome."

The policeman ordered the drinks, and the two men, both in their fifties, sat in companionable discontent as they waited. It had been a hard afternoon. A meeting of Tommaso's infernal committee. A bit of nifty footwork on Bottando's part had cut sessions down, but they had to meet sometimes. And Tommaso had worked himself into a frenzy of anxiety over his picture, demanding ever tighter security. This afternoon had been typical: a suggestion had come from Antonio Ferraro—demand was a more accurate way of describing it—that the entire building be rewired. It needed it, certainly, but, as Spello pointed out while vetoing the scheme, there wasn't enough money.

At least the machinations of museum politics had produced one pleasant change. Bottando had suggested that Ferraro might be too busy to head the museum's representation on the committee. Ferraro had agreed, evidently not liking the job, and Bottando had suggested Spello instead. The policeman felt a bit mean about this, but he was coming to sympathise with Tommaso's distaste for the sculpture expert. A very prickly character, he was unable to control a meeting without being gratuitously offensive, and had absolutely no sense that the opinions of others might have any merit at all.

The only thing to be said for Ferraro was that he exited from the committee with good grace, leaving behind only the megalomaniac, outrageously expensive, and utterly impracticable schemes he had already dreamt up; Spello was much more in tune with Bottando's disdain for committee work, and rushed through the business of killing them all off as fast as was seemly.

"So you told Tommaso he'd done it again, did you? I wish I'd been there. Preferably with a tape recorder for the amusement of my colleagues afterwards," Spello said gleefully.

"I did not tell him he'd done it again," Bottando replied testily. "I merely mentioned, in passing and during a routine check over security precautions, that someone might begin casting doubt over the authenticity of his picture."

"Was this entirely wise?" the Etruscan specialist enquired, unable to keep a broad grin off his face, despite Bottando's evident discomfort.

"No, it wasn't. In fact I told my assistant to keep it to herself. On the other hand, I don't know who Argyll knows, or who else he might talk to. I thought it best for the department—and for the museum—if Tommaso knew it might be coming, that's all."

"And like all messengers bearing bad news, you got precious little thanks for the information?"

"Mount Vesuvius in full form was nothing in comparison," Bottando said, shaking his head as he remembered the director's face turning puce and the accompanying bellow of rage. "I thought for a moment he was going to hit me. Extraordinary performance. Such a little man, as well. Who would have thought he could have made such a noise? The only time I have ever felt the slightest liking for that man Ferraro was when he intervened and tried to change the subject. Quite courageous of him, especially as I'm sure he would rather not have been there at all."

"So our Tommaso was not receptive to the idea?" prompted Spello, who would clearly have loved to hear the entire story again, for the simple pleasure of it all.

"No. Although, to give him his due, he calmed down pretty quickly, and even apologised. And told me why he was so sensitive about the matter. Although his version of the dispute over the Correggio is different from yours. In his account, he was a scapegoat slaughtered by the machinations of the dealer and the weakness of his director."

Spello sniffed. "You expected him to take full responsibility for his mistakes?"

"No. Anyway, that was a long time ago and not especially important. More significant is the fact that he's convinced that he hasn't made a mistake this time. Even gave me a huge pile of scientific tests done on the Raphael after the sale to prove it was genuine."

"You read them?"

"Not me. I'll give them to Flavia. It'll be her punishment for bringing the matter up in the first place. But Tommaso seems very confident, and he should know what he's talking about. After all, the thing has got a better pedigree than most paintings. If it came through all the tests as well, there can't be much wrong with it."

"Oh, what a pity," Spello said sadly. "You quite got my hopes up for a moment there. Still," he said, visibly brightening at the thought, "it makes a good story. Or will do," he added with a touch of malice.

"It will not. If I ever hear a word, a single breath, of this from anyone else and trace it back to you I will personally ram your finest Etruscan figurine up your nostril and glue it in place. I'm telling you for information purposes only, not so you can have a good laugh with your colleagues."

Spello looked mournful. "Oh. All right then," he said with evident reluctance. "I suppose I'll just have to hope it will turn out to be a fake. Which it will, if it is."

"Why's that?"

"Forgeries always reveal themselves eventually, that's the one great consolation about aesthetics. Or at least it's what connoisseurs convince themselves to justify the outrageously high prices of originals. What people find beautiful changes over time; you only have to look at the pale, flabby women painted by Rubens to realise that. They were reckoned to be the peak of sensuality in the seventeenth century, now they're overweight matrons; the modern age prefers the skinny Botticelli types. Even if someone paints a mock Raphael that is perfect in every detail, there will be some trace in it of the twentieth-century mind of its creator. That's the theory, anyway. As preferences change, a genuine Raphael will still look genuine, even if people see different things in it, but a modern copy will begin to show its modern origins more and more. Someone will notice. Have you ever seen those banks of Victorian fakes that most museums put on display?"

Bottando nodded.

"And what do most of the nineteenth-century hoaxes look like? Like nineteenth-century paintings, that's what. They're obviously copies to us. But to people in the nineteenth century they were beautiful examples of early Renaissance, Mannerist, Baroque art, or whatever. Do you see what I mean?"

"You seem to know a great deal about this," Bottando said.

"I'm a museum curator. Surrounded by fakes all the time. You remember those pieces in my office?" He was referring to a glass display-cabinet that Bottando had often admired. It was full of delicate, filigreed bronze figures, all Etruscan work of simple beauty and power. "Beautiful, no?" the old curator continued. Bottando nodded in agreement. "Every one a bum. Probably made in the 1930s for sale to the US. Some ended up in the museum, which wanted to melt them down when they discovered what they'd bought. I recovered them and kept them.

"I think they're wonderful. I'm an expert, so-called, and I can't tell. Only laboratory analysis proved they weren't genuine."

Bottando sniffed. "Laboratory analysis proved the Raphael was genuine," he noted.

"So, there's nothing to it. Tests are highly sophisticated these days. I must say, if I were you, I'd forget about it. Then everyone will go on enjoying the painting. Sow the tiniest seed of doubt and its popularity will wane, even if it is original. Why stir up trouble? Who has lost out anyway? As long as the museum thinks it's real, and the visitors agree, everyone's happy. And it'll take a great deal to convince our friend Tommaso, considering all the very good reasons he has to think otherwise."

Bottando laughed, turned the conversation, and put the idea from his mind. But he was uncomfortable, and his thoughts kept on returning to the subject as he walked slowly home.

THE next time Bottando saw Flavia he handed Tommaso's report to her. "There," he said. "That'll teach you. Some bedside reading for you. Photocopy it and send a copy to your mad friend in London as well, if you like. It might rein in his imagination a little."

"I'll do better. I'll give it to him this evening. He arrived in Rome yesterday, I think," she replied.

It lay on her desk for several hours as she plied her way through a host of boring chores which she always liked to get out of the way in the morning, quickly and before she was wide enough awake to resent them. When they were all done and resting contentedly in the "out" tray, she settled back into her chair, opened the report, and tried to concentrate on the harsh, technical data that was presented. A good deal of it was in the form of tables, surrounded by chemical signs which meant nothing to her. Evidently they detailed a series of tests that had been carried out.

Fortunately, there was a written introduction and conclusion, couched in the cautious language that marks both the scientist, not wanting to go beyond the limits that the evidence permits, and the bureaucrat, not wishing to stick his neck out. But the summary was clear enough.

The report began by formally detailing the project. The team, the permanent employees of the Museo Nazionale, had been sent to London to examine a painting, "supposed to be by Raphael," and determine its authenticity. They had been given free use of the apparatus at the National Gallery in London, as well as assistance from employees at the Tate. The tests had lasted a week which, they said, was more than enough time to make all the experiments they thought necessary. They noted, cautiously, that their work was of limited utility. They did not intend to comment on the aesthetic merits or otherwise of the painting.

"Just as well," thought Flavia, remembering the dry technocrat who had ruled supreme for years at the museum. "Without a spectrometer they couldn't tell a Botticelli from a Chagall."

She flipped through the pages of experiments and began on the conclusion, on the safe assumption that whatever the main body of the text contained would be duplicated in simpler language at the end.

The examiners had begun by looking at the canvas. This, they said, consisted of threads of varying width with irregular weaving, consistent with the canvases used in the late fifteenth century. The stretch-marks indicated that the canvas had not been cut down or stretched on to a new frame, and the wooden frame itself, made of poplar, also appeared to be of an appropriate age. A carbon-fibre dating of the canvas and the paint—done by snipping a miniscule fragment off the side, grinding it down and dosing it with radioactivity—indicated that it was not less than three hundred and fifty years old.

"Before 1600, more or less. Pre-Mantini, in other words," she noted. So far the picture was holding up well.

The experts had then moved on to the paintwork itself, noting that as the picture had been covered over for more than two hundred years and had been cleaned and restored before examination, there were particular difficulties. They also noted that they had been instructed to keep any paint removed for analysis to the absolute minimum, and come from as near to the edges as possible. However, the report continued that, despite these strictures, they were able to complete a fairly full examination of the different colours used and of the techniques employed in painting.

Again, the portrait came through. The craquelure, the hairline cracks that appear in old oil paintings as they age and grow brittle, were irregular; artificially induced cracks generally ran parallel as a forger rolled the picture up to give a false impression of age. The remains of dirt in the cracks—most had been cleaned out—were composed of different substances while forgeries generally contained some homogeneous material, such as ink, used to give the impression of dirt.

All the paints were of raw materials used in the sixteenth century and X-ray examination, conducted at different electricity levels to build up a three-dimensional picture down through the paint, suggested that it had been painted according to techniques used in other Raphael works.

The final summary was as definite as any scientist was likely to be. Under examination and bearing in mind the limitations mentioned, the painting was consistent with a work produced at the start of the sixteenth century by a painter using techniques also employed in several of Raphael's works. The lengthy footnote, with citations, detailed the virtual impossibility of reproducing such characteristics in a modern picture. Of course, judgement was reserved on whether it actually was by Raphael, but there was not a shred of evidence to suggest that it was not. The report was dated and signed by all five members of the investigating team.

Flavia put the folder down, rubbed her eyes and stretched herself. That, certainly, seemed to nobble Argyll's suspicions. She turned her attention to the mound of mail that had built up on her desk while she was reading, and started methodically but absent-mindedly to transfer most of the envelopes to the desk of the temporarily absent Paolo. Her work was, perhaps, thirty per cent enjoyable and seventy per cent dull and routine. Running around interviewing people, tracing pictures, keeping up contacts among dealers, auctioneers and collectors was the fun part. Reading reports, checking journals and filling out the innumerable forms that the polizia considered a vital aspect of good security work was very much less so. A nice, juicy scandal would have tipped the balance more towards the entertaining end. Pity.

7

ANY lingering regret on the subject of Elisabetta in Flavia's mind had only until 10:37 the following Thursday to germinate before being consigned to the distant past.

She knew that it was exactly 10:37, because that was the time stamp that the ancient telex machine in the office placed at the end of the message from the French police saying that the case of the icon-stealing tourist had reached a conclusion, albeit not a very satisfactory one. The message from Paris read that Jean-Luc Morneau, connoisseur, aesthete, painter, dealer and suspected criminal, had been found. Unfortunately, he was dead, and so was likely to be of little use in helping the police with their enquiries.

The French were quite proud of their discovery although, as Bottando observed, they appeared to have no idea where all the icons had gone. The fact that Morneau had clearly died of a heart attack, brought on, so the Parisians said discreetly, by excess exertion, lessened Bottando's interest. Especially as there was a witness to both the exertions and the demise, and the graphic details provided by the young woman involved were convincing enough to rule out foul play. Bottando was not greatly concerned in the matter, as he had long since given up hope that any of the missing Italian icons would ever be discovered. But, for the sake of thoroughness, he asked the French to keep his department informed about any new developments.

In due course, the French ran the dealer's old mistress to earth. In return for their agreeing to ignore the state of her income-tax payments, she told them that Morneau had rented a safe deposit box in a Swiss bank. A bit of gentle arm-twisting of opposite numbers in Zurich produced a grudging permission to look inside it, and Bottando was invited to come along to the grand opening.

Six weeks to the day after Morneau's body was discovered, therefore, Bottando and Flavia flew into Zurich airport, where they were met by an official police car and driven swiftly into the financial heart of the city. As usual, Bottando had wanted to stay in Rome and grumbled incessantly during the flight. If he disliked travelling, he disliked travelling to Switzerland even more. The cleanliness, order and efficiency of the place profoundly upset him and he also found the Swiss insufferable, not least because of his utter failure to persuade them to do anything to stop the steady flow of smuggled art works over the Italian/ Swiss border.

The only thing that persuaded him to get on the plane, in fact, was the realisation that it was an ideal excuse for not going to yet another of Tommaso's parties in the museum. Its purpose was uncertain, but the man had said something about fund raising and was insisting that all members of the Security Committee, as it was now grandly termed, were present. Bottando took considerable pleasure in ringing up, presenting his apologies, and pleading pressing police business.

Tommaso had not been happy. He was angling for a large donation, he said, and really needed Bottando there to impress the potential benefactors. It was only when Bottando explained, with some exaggeration, that he needed to go to Switzerland and had high hopes of recovering some invaluable icons, that the man gave way.

He did it, at least, with some grace. If Bottando could recover any part of the Italian heritage, then that must take precedence, he said somewhat pompously. The General should not even consider coming to the party. They would manage without him, and Spello would be there to answer any questions about museum security.

So he'd gone, and had slowly begun to wonder whether the museum folk were worse than the Swiss police, or the other way around. Attempts at international conversation as the large black Mercedes whistled down the autobahn were accordingly muted, and the atmosphere did not thaw until Bottando spotted his long-time French equivalent in the bank lobby.

Jean Janet was universally liked. One of the rare French protestants, he hailed from the Alsace region in the east of the country, and had headed his department before Bottando's position had even been a twinkle in a bureaucrat's eye. In the early years he had been unfailingly helpful in getting the Roman sezione into working order, illicitly handing over vast files of material, introducing Bottando to influential and knowledgeable gossip-mongers in the art world, passing on advice on some of the more subtle aspects of police work in the art field. Bottando had, in turn, gone out of his way to be helpful whenever possible. Any request from Janet was treated as a high-priority matter, and the direct and easygoing exchange of material had proved beneficial to both sides.

Apart from that, Bottando genuinely liked the man's sense of humour, and Paris had become one of the few places outside Italy that he travelled to willingly. Janet's only real disadvantage, apart from powerful halitosis, was that he refused to speak anything but French, and this limited conversation. Especially as Bottando was an equally idle linguist—although he could become positively fluent after a good meal and a cognac.

He stumbled through his greeting, again acutely conscious of what he was sure were the contemptuous eyes of the bilingual Swiss policemen, and made up for it by wringing his friend's hand firmly and beaming at him.

"I am delighted to see you once more, my friend," said Janet. "What do you think of our little bit of detective work, eh? And even," he added, waving his hand at the still silent Swiss, "persuading these secretive folk to let us look in one of the vaults! Not bad for an old Frenchman."

As they were led down the stairs and through a series of gleaming steel gates towards the deposit boxes, Bottando congratulated his colleague on his swiftness and fortune. "Fortune, poof! Good police work. Research, interviews, careful questioning. Well, perhaps some luck. But only a little."

Bottando confessed that he didn't think there would be much in the box to interest him. "After all, our icons disappeared nine years ago. The chances of him having kept one as a souvenir are a bit slight—even if he did take them."

"I, also, do not expect a treasure trove. But who knows? It is a pity he died so inconsiderately. A brief conversation would have been very interesting."

Playing the Gallic extrovert with gusto, a role he habitually adopted when dealing with any sort of foreigner, Janet rubbed his hands together with theatrical anticipation as the heavily armed security guard took out a key and inserted it in the door of a large steel box, one of about a hundred in the room they had entered. Bottando noted that most of the owners were probably under the impression that theirs was the only key to their box, and that whatever they chose to keep in it was absolutely safe from either theft or, sometimes worse, examination. Another example of Swiss duplicity, he thought.

Morneau's box was about two feet square and three feet long, with a door of angled sheet steel two inches thick. As one of the Swiss policemen had told them on the way down, it was one of the most expensive types he could have rented, and cost ten thousand Swiss francs a year. That in itself, he added, suggested that there should be something interesting inside.

He was wrong. There were no stolen icons, no convenient address books containing the names of icon collectors, no sets of accounts detailing payments received, nothing at all that would get the investigation any further along. But there was a lot of money: some half million Swiss francs, at least fifty thousand dollars in small denomination notes, and the same amount again in Deutschmarks and sterling. All in all, about four hundred thousand dollars in loose currency. Apart from that, the only contents were a bundle of sketchbooks, well-thumbed and spattered with blobs of paint, bound up with a length of red tape. While the money was being taken out and counted, and sets of serial numbers taken down so that attempts could be made to trace their origin, Flavia sat down in a quiet corner—she had been largely ignored all morning and had barely spoken a word since they landed—and flicked through the sketchbooks.

Some of them were clearly many years old, and were full of details of arms and legs, different types of faces and costume, the sort of thing that every art student at one of the more traditional painting academies is required to turn out. She remembered that, in the thirties, Morneau had been at the prestigious *Académie des Beaux Arts* in Paris and had made the beginnings of a promising career as a painter before turning to the more financially rewarding business of dealing. He had also taught in Lyons before going commercial. As she looked at the sketches with a critical eye, she could see why. He was very skilled, and the line drawings particularly were executed with ease and dexterity. But they were old-fashioned in the extreme, and almost entirely derivative. Dredging up the remnants of her education, she spotted drawings after Rembrandt, legs copied from Parmigianino, endless repetitions of fragments from the Sistine Chapel, all done with minute changes as the artist experimented to see what the painters had been doing.

Intermingled with the sketches were voluminous jottings. The notes were probably part of the dreary lectures in art history that were churned out until the riots of 1968 produced a revolution in methods. The new way didn't produce any better painters, but it was probably less boring. Recipes for paints, quotations from artists, extracts from books on techniques, all written in a fast, ill-formed hand that was often barely legible. The other books, many in better condition than the first, were of the same type. The newest were the three at the top of the pile and, once more, followed the same pattern.

Flavia decided that recognition of painterly style was merely a matter of keeping the eye practised. In the first volume she examined she had had to concentrate hard to tell even Rubens from Correggio. Now, after only a few minutes, the recognition was coming much faster and more easily.

She looked again, concentrating hard, and then glanced up to confirm that the five men were still busy talking to each other and were ignoring her very existence. She slipped three of the books in the black leather handbag that everyone in her office always made fun of for being so absurdly large and unladylike, bound the rest in the red cotton tape, and replaced them on the table with the bundles of money.

FORTY-FIVE minutes later, the two Italians and the Frenchman were sitting in a restaurant ordering food. Lunch had been Flavia's idea, and it had been taken up enthusiastically by her superiors, if for different reasons. There had been a polite disagreement about where to go. Janet had suggested an Italian trattoria, Bottando had returned the compliment by insisting that they go French. Because he was very much of the opinion that this was by far the best decision, Janet had let himself be persuaded, but made up for his chauvinism by ordering a bottle of Montepulciano, which he considered one of the few Italian wines that might deservedly have been produced in his home country.

He took an appreciative sip then asked, "Well, my friends, and what is it that I can do for you?"

Bottando looked surprised. "For us? What makes you think we want something?"

"I do apologise, but I'm sure one of you does. I am a thoughtful person, and observant. And I know you well. You are a polite man, and you were very rude in disposing of those Swiss so that you could eat alone in my company. I am flattered, and I know your opinion of our Swiss colleagues. But you could have asked me earlier and made it less obvious. So, I think to myself, you want to ask me something that has only just occurred to you. And the invitation came after that whispering in your ear from your assistant here. Therefore . . ."

"Entirely incorrect. I just wanted to enjoy my lunch rather than have to suffer through it. Although I must admit I do want to hear what you know about Morneau. He sounds a character."

"He was. I recommend, by the way, the trout. It comes with one of the few sauces they do here which doesn't have too much flour. Otherwise, stick to the veal. It is very good to see you again. But, I must insist that you play fair. I will tell you about the life and secret career of Monsieur Morneau—as much as we know—if you tell me the latest goings-on and scandal in Rome. I haven't seen you for some time. There must be a great deal I've missed."

He fussed over the bread, spearing it on his fork and using it to sop up some garlic sauce from his plate, while Bottando considered whether he should break the policy of silence about the Raphael which he had so convincingly explained to Flavia several weeks back. It was about the only decent anecdote of recent vintage, and he knew Janet would appreciate it. On the other hand, he doubted the man's ability to keep it to himself.

"Well, then," Janet began, lifting his head reluctantly from his plate and wiping a dribble of gravy from his chin. "As you probably noticed, Morneau was an exceedingly rich man for an art dealer. He had an extravagant lifestyle, a house in Provence, a spacious apartment in Paris, and a gallery which, although successful, certainly did not generate enough income to support his expenditure. No mortgages, no debts. All his residences, incidentally, had been completely swept of any incriminating papers by the time we got there to have a look around. A very tidy man.

"So where did this money come from? Not from legitimate activities, and not from peddling stolen icons either. We know of twenty-five he probably stole. Even if there are another twenty-five we don't know about, that gives you, say, six or seven million francs over a ten-year period. He spent much more than that. So what else was he up to?

"Then he disappears. This is a man who turns up at almost every gallery opening, hasn't missed a performance of the ballet for nearly fifteen years, and is an artistic socialite of the first order. He ducks out of sight for nearly a year, and then he turns up, in an embarrassing position and dead. So where has he been, eh? Tell me that."

He finished his little speech and smiled, as if expecting applause for the brilliance of his logic.

"I was hoping *you* would. You haven't actually told us anything at all. What was he doing?" Bottando asked.

Janet shrugged. "There I cannot help you. Deduction can take you only so far. Any further requires more information. Now tell me. What about Rome?"

Before he could begin, Flavia, who had been staring absently out of the window, made one of her first comments of the day. She didn't like being ignored, although she was occasionally prepared to put up with being treated as merely a decorative appendage by Bottando. He didn't do it very often and, besides, he was old and southern and could hardly be expected to be perfect. But it was time, she decided, to make her presence felt.

"Maybe we should test the Commissioner's powers of deduction a little further," she said, smiling winsomely at the Frenchman. She always did that when she suspected she might be being a little rude. But before she could proceed further along these lines, Bottando interrupted her.

"Quite," he said. "But how good a painter was he? What were those fake icons he turned out like? It struck me that we might approach some of the more reputable forgers in Naples and ask a few careful questions there. Now he's dead they would probably be more forthcoming than usual."

Janet considered the matter for a moment. "As for Morneau's qualities as a painter, he was very good indeed, but he was born too late. He disliked modernism in all its forms. Had he been born a century earlier he would have had a great success.

"His icons were very variable. The earliest ones were good, painted on old panels, covered in dirt, quite well-executed. But once the technicians knew what they were looking for, they could easily spot them—something about paint in wormholes, which you don't get in the real thing. The later ones were sloppy. It looks as though he realised that they didn't really have to be that good to be convincing, so stopped wasting so much effort.

"Technical problems aside, however, they are remarkable, even the bad ones. They have a great spiritual quality, almost as if he were painting for his own sake. I'm not really surprised the monks were taken in. Once they had been aged and covered with dirt, they looked wonderful, even better than the originals. You should see them. One always tends to assume that fakes are not as good as the real thing. I'm not so sure. Morneau understood the paintings. That's where most of these people fall down." He smiled at the two of them. "There. All along you suspected your old friend was a Philistine, eh?"

They had reached the coffee, and the conversation showed signs of wandering off into the byways and alleyways of anecdote. Flavia stirred herself for another attempt.

"Commissioner," she began. "The bank's log of when Morneau opened his box. When was the last visit?"

"I don't know. We haven't been able to get that out of the bank yet. However, according to his passport, he last visited Switzerland in May," he answered.

She smiled in quiet triumph. She must remember to

point out to Bottando what an extraordinarily good employee she was. Even if she occasionally caused him a great deal of trouble and heartache. As she was about to do now. She reached into her handbag and took out one of the sketchbooks she'd purloined. Apologising insincerely for abducting evidence in such a cavalier fashion, she handed it across to the two men. "Have a look at that. Ring any bells?" she asked.

Janet glanced at it, looked noncommittally puzzled, and passed it to Bottando. He was equally blank. Then Flavia detected vague stirrings of unease, and a sudden realisation. "Ah," he said as he handed it back. Very quick on the uptake, really, she thought.

"I don't mean to be inquisitive . . ." Janet said.

Bottando looked flustered. "Indeed not," he said. "But this must be kept very quiet. The slightest hint could wreak havoc on the market."

Flavia was again impressed. She'd had the entire walk to the restaurant to work out the implications of the discovery; Bottando had had only a few seconds and he instantly saw the problems and pitfalls. Especially the impact on the art market if the slightest breath slipped out.

"Of course, of course," replied Janet. "But what is it, exactly, that I'm not meant to hint about?"

Flavia handed him back the notebook. "These sketches," she said casually, "would appear to bear a remarkably strong resemblance to the portrait of Elisabetta di Laguna in Rome. By Raphael. Or perhaps we'd better begin to say, *attributed* to Raphael."

Janet looked again, then nodded. "I suppose they do. But so what? Every artist in the western world has probably made sketches of it."

"Before last May? Before the painting had been uncovered and before anyone could possibly have known what it looked like?"

Janet leaned back in his seat, and a broad smile slowly spread across his face. "How splendid," he commented eventually. "How delightful," he said after further thought. "How very awkward for you," he added apologetically as an afterthought.

"When you've stopped enjoying yourself," Bottando said severely, "you'll begin to see why it's important you keep very quiet. No gossip back in the office. Not a word. Not even to your wife. Or anybody."

"Oh, quite. Quite. But please, I beg you. Clear this one up quickly. Every day without telling someone will be a day wasted. And, of course," he added, with some attempt to return to professionalism, "any help you need of me, just let me know.

"Oh dear," he said, his face cracking with pleasure once more, "I wish I could be there when you tell that awful man Tommaso."

"Everybody says that," said Bottando gloomily. "But I'm the one who is going to have to face him. I may not survive the blast."

The meal ended shortly after that, Janet heading back

for France in good humour and with a promise to send on the log when he'd got it out of the Swiss. Bottando's spirits were considerably lower. Before they boarded the plane that was to fly them home from Zurich to Rome at four o'clock that afternoon, he phoned the museum and asked to speak to the director. He was in a meeting, and a secretary, clearly briefed to deflect all unforeseen calls, declined to bring him to the phone, even though Bottando insisted that it was an important matter and police business.

Bottando gave up the struggle. He'd have to go to the party after all, and catch him there. The worst of both worlds, he thought morosely.

8

ONCE he arrived at the museum in the Borghese gardens, Bottando handed in his coat and made his way along to the ground-floor gallery where the reception was taking place. It was a big affair, well under way by the time he got there, and the main sculpture gallery had been thrown open to accommodate the dozens of guests. He took a glass of champagne from a passing waiter, noting that, as usual, Tommaso was deploying what he always claimed were scarce museum funds in a lavish fashion.

"Not at all," replied a museum member who had zeroed in on the same tray of drinks and to whom Bottando made this somewhat cynical comment. "Tommaso calls it investment. He has a point, in fact. This bash is in honour of those gentlemen over there." He pointed towards a group of half a dozen men leaning on a large statue.

"Doesn't anyone mind them using a Canova as a drinks trolley?" enquired Bottando. He looked at the group closely. They had all just come in to the room with the director, and were standing around one of the giant statues in the middle of the gallery. All wore light-grey suits, blue shirts and striped ties. They were talking intensely, and Bottando suspected they were not discussing the artistic beauties which lay all around them.

"Certainly not. You see, they're American businessmen who are hoping to win a government defence contract." The man made an expansive gesture which was meant to give an impression of gigantic wealth and the machinations that go along with it. It was a broad sweep of the arm, not very well co-ordinated. Bottando decided he'd been drinking.

"And what better way of creating the right impression than making a large donation to the national museum," Bottando finished for him. The young man, in his thirties with an open countenance that was currently shaded by alcoholic distress, nodded firmly.

"Exactly. Their big white chief is currently locked in discussion with Tommaso in his office. To be followed, no doubt, by a large cheque which will cover the cost of the party and leave a considerable amount over to deal with the abominable electrical circuits in this run-down old dump. Clever, eh?"

Bottando turned towards him. "Do you know," he

said, "I think that you're the first person in this place who's ever said a positive word about Tommaso."

The man's face clouded. "Giulio Manzoni, by the way," he offered, holding out a hand which Bottando briefly shook. "Deputy restorer. I admit he's not liked. But he's really not as bad as he seems. And this place needed an awful good shake to knock some of the dust out. Not that my relatively favourable opinion will do me much good, alas."

"Meaning?"

"You weren't here earlier? Evidently not. He's gone and resigned. Said he's decided to take early retirement and go to live in his house in Tuscany. A bit of a shock, all things considered. As you no doubt know, everything in this place is done through patronage. My job, for instance, came through the assistance of Enrico Spello and I'm seen very much as his protégé."

"That's good, isn't it?" Bottando enquired, a little taken aback by the news. "I mean, Spello is next in line."

The restorer shook his head matter of factly. "Not any more, he isn't. Because Tommaso at the same time appointed Ferraro as his successor and official deputy."

"Goodness," said Bottando mildly as he considered the implications. "I thought he couldn't stand Ferraro. What prompted this?"

"Perhaps he's sick of being disliked. Maybe he's human after all. Besides, he's gigantically rich, so why crack your head working? He does dislike Ferraro, but evidently he dislikes Spello more. You can never tell with him; it's difficult to penetrate the façade. Besides, the only way people will look on his passing with regret is to make sure his successor is even more unpleasant than he is. You see why I'm heading for my fifth drink of the evening?"

Bottando nodded sagely. "I think so," he replied.

"You think so? Well, let me show you, so there's no mistake." Manzoni leant forward and poked Bottando in the chest. "Ferraro is a little rat, right? Spello will be his main rival. So he wants to chop Spello down to size, whittle away at his support. He can't attack Spello himself, as he's got tenure. So how will he get at him? Through me, that's how." He now poked himself on the chest to emphasise the point, then turned and gesticulated at the new deputy director, coming through the tall oak doors on the far side of the room.

"Look at him. He has the air of triumph on his face, don't you think? A man who has just conquered all. An air of vulgar triumph."

"Are you sure the appointment will go through? After all, it's not Tommaso's personal gift." So far, Bottando was finding the conversation decidedly upsetting. He had, on the whole, relatively few dealings with the museum. Although he never felt entirely comfortable with Tommaso, the two had at least worked out a *modus vivendi* so that life did not become too onerous. He doubted that Ferraro would be quite so easy.

Manzoni nodded, his aggressive mood swiftly fading into one of lugubrious resignation. "A few months back the succession would have been close. Spello would have been the inside candidate; the reconciler, someone everybody could work with. Then, of course, Tommaso pulls off his *coup de théâtre* with that Raphael and everyone in government thinks he's the greatest thing since sliced salami. Whoever he supports will walk in now."

The restorer looked extremely upset, and stared at his again empty glass. Then, without a further word, he shambled off in the direction of the drinks trolley. Bottando breathed a sigh of relief; sympathetic though he felt, he had other things to worry about at the moment.

But Tommaso wasn't around; that he realised as he surveyed the room in search of him. In one corner he saw Spello, and could tell by the man's slightly stooped shoulders that he was feeling very disappointed, and probably angry as well. He sympathised, but wasn't in the mood to listen to another outburst of indignation, no matter how justifiable. In another corner he spotted Jonathan Argyll and Sir Edward Byrnes. He was momentarily surprised that either should be there, and that such an evidently amiable conversation could take place, but then remembered Flavia mentioning Argyll's fellowship. There is nothing like a little money to soothe the passions. They, at least, seemed in a good mood, but he felt disinclined to talk to anyone even remotely connected with that Raphael. So, he spent the next ten minutes being talked at by some connoisseur and critic, while mainly keeping his eyes open, waiting for Tommaso's reappearance.

Eventually the door swung open, revealing a cameo of Tommaso shaking hands with the senior American and evidently bidding him farewell. The gracious look on his face suggested he'd got his cheque. Bottando waited for the right moment to go up and ruin his evening. He didn't want another public explosion on his hands.

He was staring idly around him, uncertain about what to do, and the indecision lost him his chance to catch the director on his own and escape home early. Ferraro had also materialised at the doorway and had engaged the man in an earnest conversation. Even at a distance of many metres, Bottando could see the expression of benign good humour drain out of the director's face like water out of an unplugged bath. It would be an exaggeration to say that he turned green, but a sickly shade of off-white was well within the bounds of accuracy. Ferraro, in contrast, looked in control of himself but decidedly grim.

He was spared the trouble of having to go over and find out what was so evidently distressing to both men. Tommaso walked swiftly over to him, the air of effortless grace still present in his every step despite the look of concern on his face. Perhaps he hadn't got the money after all?

"General. I'm glad to see you," he said shortly, leaving out, for once, the elaborate courtesies he habitually employed. "Could you come with me, please. I've just had a piece of shocking news."

The director set off at a fast clip through the museum, along the entrance hall and up the stairs. Bottando puffed along to keep up. "What is the matter?" he asked, but got no reply. Tommaso looked as though he had just seen a ghost. Ferraro was unusually silent as well.

There was no need for complex explanations. As they opened the door and went into one of the smaller galleries on the second floor, it was immediately clear what the matter was.

"Mother of God," said Bottando quietly.

The frame of the Raphael was still there, badly charred in its upper parts, but nobody could ever have suspected that the few blackened threads and dark congealed liquid that hung loosely from it had been, until very recently, the most expensive and treasured painting in the world.

Four or five square inches of the bottom right-hand side, Bottando estimated, had been untouched by the fire, which had reduced the rest of the canvas to charred rubbish. The smell of burning oil, wood, and material, still hung in the air, and wisps of smoke rose from the few pieces of cloth that had not been entirely consumed. Above the picture, the wallpaper was badly charred, and had evidently come close to catching fire as well. Bottando found time to be thankful the museum had not decorated the room with padded silk, as they occasionally did. If they had, the whole building would have been ablaze by now.

None of the three said anything at all, but simply looked. Bottando saw very grave difficulties, Tomasso the ruin of his reputation, Ferraro the end of his ambitions. "No," said Tommaso, and that was all. For the first time, Bottando felt sorry for the man.

Memory of his occupation reasserted itself. "Who found it?" he asked quietly.

"I did," said Ferraro. "Just now. I came back down immediately to tell the director and found him by the door."

"What were you doing in here?"

"I was going up to my office to get a packet of cigarettes. And I saw smoke coming from under the door. I knew something was wrong the moment I smelt it."

"Why?"

"No fire alarm. It's very sensitive. We turned it off for the rooms where the party was being held, but it should have been on for every other room."

Bottando grunted and looked around. It required no great genius to see what had happened. He crouched down by an aerosol tin on the floor, not touching it. Engine starter. High-grade petrol you squirt into carburettors to start the car on cold days. Spray the picture, push a lit match against it, leave and shut the door behind you. The fuel lit up the dry but still inflammable paint on the canvas, and the whole thing was burnt away within minutes. He looked at the picture once more. Someone right-handed, he guessed. He seemed to have sprayed in an arc from bottom left to top right. Hence the relative lack of damage in the bottom right-hand corner. He lightly and cautiously touched the remains hanging in the frame. Still warm.

He sighed, and turned to Ferraro.

"Close this door and put a guard on it. Go downstairs,

tell them the party's over but no one is to leave. Don't say what's happened. We've enough to do at the moment without worrying about the press. I will phone for reinforcements. Perhaps we can use your office, director?"

BOTTANDO spent another three hours there, dealing with the more stratospheric consequences of the evening's events. Phoning his colleagues in other departments, informing the arts minister, mustering his forces. He occupied the desk, while Tommaso fretted around, summoning assistants and public relations officials to draft a release to give to the press. Despite Bottando's strictures, they had already sensed something had happened, and they would have to be told sooner or later.

It was some time before the policeman and the director had time to talk. Tommaso was sitting listlessly on the ornate nineteenth-century sofa, staring at a Flemish painting on the opposite wall as though he'd suddenly discovered it was a personal enemy.

"Do you have any idea why the fire alarm didn't work?" the policeman asked him.

"The usual reasons, I imagine," Tommaso replied with a barely concealed groan. "The electrical system in this place is a menace. Hasn't been changed since the 1940s. We're lucky the entire museum hasn't burnt down. That's why I submitted the proposal to have the place rewired to the security committee. It's a pity Spello vetoed it."

"Hmm," replied Bottando noncommittally. He picked

up the double implication clearly. Spello had made this attack possible by stopping the proposal. Secondly, it wouldn't take much manoeuvring to divert any blame for the destruction from the director to the committee.

That would have to be dealt with later. He concentrated instead on the matter at hand. "How often does the thing shut down?"

"Constantly. Well, about once a week. The last time was in the evening a couple of days ago. Ferraro was still here, fortunately. He had to pull all the fuses out to stop the entire building from burning down. The guards had gone off to the bar, as usual. It really is like trying to run a madhouse in here, at times," he added with some considerable despair. Bottando sympathised. He could imagine.

"Anyway," the director continued, "that, indirectly, was the point of this party. I persuaded those Americans to hand over a donation that was going to rewire the entire building. Thus overcoming Spello's prejudices about modernisation." He laughed bitterly. "Shutting the stable after the horse has bolted, if you like. I imagine they'll cancel the cheque."

"Was this problem generally known?"

"Oh yes. The bell going off at random all the time is not the sort of thing you can keep secret. Oh. I see what you mean. This indicates it was done by someone inside the museum, you think?"

Bottando shrugged. "Not necessarily. But I think we

should go and have a look at that fuse box. Could you show me where it is?"

A few minutes and several flights of stairs later, they were standing in the basement. "There you are," said Tommaso. He opened the gigantic, rusty box on the wall. Inside was line upon line of heavy ceramic fuses. He searched around, pulled one out, looked at it, and handed it to Bottando. "Thought so. Blown again," he commented.

Bottando held it up to the light and looked, a favourite theory evaporating as he did so. No one had removed the fuse, no one had cut any wires. It had just burnt through of its own accord. Only in Italy, he thought to himself, would things be done in such a ramshackle fashion. He found himself beginning to have more sympathy with Tommaso's reformist efforts. Tactful, he wasn't. But no one could say there wasn't a job to be done here.

In such a conciliatory spirit, once back in the director's office, the General tentatively began to raise the subject that had brought him to the party in the first place.

"There are one or two aspects of all this I thought it would be best to discuss with you alone. It might take some of the sting out of this appalling evening."

The director placed the tips of his fingers together, and peered at him enquiringly. He didn't appear to believe anything could do that.

"I don't think your loss today was as grievous as it seems," Bottando continued.

The director grimaced and shook his head. "I assure

you, the painting is beyond repair. Or perhaps you don't find the loss of one of the greatest triumphs of Italian art grievous?"

A bit pompous, thought Bottando uncharitably. Still, he has had a bad day. "A triumph, certainly. But not of Italian art. I think it was a forgery."

Tommaso snorted. "Oh, General, not this obsession of yours again. I've already told you it's impossible. You know as well as I do the tests that picture went through. It passed them all with flying colours. And every scholar in the field pronounced it to be a Raphael."

"Experts can be wrong. Every scholar in the world in the 1930s said the *Supper at Emmaus* was by Vermeer. They only discovered it was painted by Van Meegeren when he confessed to avoid being hanged for collaboration with the Nazis."

"The fake Vermeers were detected easily when they were examined scientifically," Tommaso objected. "And techniques have improved immeasurably since the 1940s."

"So, no doubt, have the forger's. But this is neither here nor there. The evidence we have is circumstantial, but worrying enough."

"And what, pray, is your evidence?"

Bottando reminded him about the letter found by Argyll in the country-house muniments room. The director interrupted. "But this is no less feeble now than before. You surely don't expect the entire academic community to change its mind on the basis of that?"

"Indeed not. As you say, on its own the letter amounts

to very little. However, earlier today, my assistant found something a bit more convincing, hence my telephone call from Zurich to that infuriatingly obstructive secretary of yours."

He briefly told the director about the hunt for Morneau, the safe deposit box and their discovery.

That clearly rattled Tommaso. He walked across to a shelf of leather-bound books, swung it open and took out a bottle. He poured some golden liquid into two glasses and handed one to Bottando. He swilled it around and rubbed his face with his free hand. All his pomposity had evaporated again.

"If I understand you correctly, your argument hinges only on those date stamps in that passport? Someone else could have put those drawings in the safe deposit *after* the painting was splashed over every magazine and newspaper in the country?"

Bottando dipped his head in acknowledgement. "Yes. I told you it was circumstantial. But we now have two fragments pointing at the same thing."

"I really don't believe this," the director said eventually. "And if it was true, why would anyone bother to destroy the painting? I mean," he said defiantly, "it's obvious why this happened, isn't it?"

Bottando gazed at him enquiringly.

"This was an attack on me, clearly. Only today I said I was retiring, and that Ferraro would succeed. Destroying the picture was a retaliation, to make me look a fool. It only makes sense if the picture was genuine. I know I'm not popular here."

He paused. Bottando wondered whether he was expected to demur and reassure the director on that score. But he decided even Tommaso wasn't that vain, so he kept quiet.

"Everybody has always resented what I've tried to do, tried to stop every improvement I've introduced. Ferraro is the only one here who's given me any support at all. The only one who doesn't live somewhere back in the 1920s."

"Hence the preference for him over Spello?"

"Yes. I like Spello, and I don't like Ferraro much. But the future of the museum is at stake, and I could see no room for personal preference." Again, just a shade of the old pomposity peeked through his suddenly energetic explanations.

"Spello is a good deputy, but the director has to fight with the ministries, squeeze money out of donors. I decided that only Ferraro could do it. He's not an easy man, I admit, but he's the best possible choice I had. And there are a lot of people who'd be prepared to stop me and him. At any cost."

It was a legitimate interpretation, Bottando conceded. "But," he objected, "I find it difficult to see how anyone who'd worked in a museum all their life could ever bring themselves to such an act of vandalism."

"Don't you believe it," Tommaso snorted. "I said this was a madhouse and I meant it. But don't you get the point of what I'm saying?" he continued intensely, staring at the policeman and leaning forward on his chair in an effort to convince him, "If that picture was a fake, why destroy it? It would be much better to leave it and have the fraud discovered."

Bottando smiled and shifted his conversational rudder a little to the right. "If that painting was a fake, everyone was fooled by it, not just you. If Italy hadn't bought it, the Getty would have. Or someone else. The psychology of its appearance was just right, so no one thought to doubt it. All the evidence suggested there should be a picture under that Mantini. Byrnes produces it. It was like a fairy tale. Everyone wanted to believe it. Perhaps even the man who burnt it believed it was genuine."

Tommaso smiled wanly. "But it was us who paid out the money. The fact that others would have done so, given the chance, is a relatively small compensation, compared to the damage to my reputation."

There was little else Bottando wanted to discuss, so he got up and made his way to the door. He was tired as well. "Tell me," he said casually as he was leaving, "why did you decide to quit? I confess I was very surprised."

"So was everybody. I enjoyed seeing their faces when the announcement went out. Too much of the ambitious careerist, they thought. But I've had enough of this job and I don't need the money. All administration and backbiting. It needs a younger man." Tommaso smiled curiously.

"Hence Ferraro?"

"Yes. He's very able, despite his unfortunate manner, and knows how to spot an opportunity. He ran the place for a few weeks a year ago. He made some good moves then. It was that which got him the job.

"As for me," he continued in a melancholy voice, "I plan to go off to my villa outside Pienza and live quietly with my library and my collection. Who knows? I may take up painting myself again. I haven't done any for years. It'll be a pleasant change—especially now. You must admit my timing is impeccable. Or someone else's is."

He opened the door and shook Bottando's hand.

"I know we've never been easy colleagues, General," he said. "But I'd like you to know that I appreciate your efforts to find the man who did this. All I ask is that you suppress this rumour of a fake. If you come up with real proof, that's another matter. But I will not stand for my reputation being dragged through the mud because of a bizarre hunch."

Bottando nodded. "That's reasonable. And we have our own reasons for keeping quiet. Don't worry. Good night, director."

WHILE Bottando was being grudgingly impressed by Tommaso's reaction to the evening's catastrophe, Flavia, on his orders, was wading her way through the drudge work that is inevitably associated with crime.

It was too late to do formal interviews of all eighty-seven people at the reception. She merely took their names and addresses, and asked them, politely but with authority, to remain within easy reach. She then passed the list on to immigration on the off-chance that someone would try to cross the border. It didn't seem likely. The only ones she missed were the group of Americans, who had already left by a late flight from the airport. However, they seemed the least likely suspects.

And suspects, she thought, they had enough of already; and some of them were clearly smart enough to realise where they stood. Argyll, for instance, who came in almost last.

"I'd rather hoped I would only ever see you socially in future. I never thought you'd be interrogating me again," he said wistfully.

"I'm not interrogating. Just getting your address," she replied in her stern manner.

He waved his hand. "A mere detail. You will be. After all, I must be your top suspect."

"You flatter yourself."

"Not really. Oh, all right. Maybe not number one. But in the top five, certainly. I can't say I like it much."

Flavia leaned back in her seat and put her feet on the desk. She was tired, and it was difficult to remain entirely hard and professional with someone you knew and liked. Besides, she wasn't in the police, so didn't have to. Sometimes that gave her an advantage.

"If you're so sure, perhaps you should give me your reasoning?"

He looked up at the ceiling for a moment to arrange his thoughts. "You think that picture was a fake, correct?" he began.

"What makes you think that?"

He shrugged. "Must be. Either that or you're looking for a maniac."

Flavia said nothing.

"If it was, of course," Argyll continued, "Byrnes received umpteen million for a dud. Which I, incidentally, first discovered. An accomplishment I am now beginning to regret. And I am now associated with Byrnes through his fellowship."

He paused, so she prompted, "So why fry the thing?"

"Because when it's discovered and proven to be a fake, Byrnes would have to take it back and refund the money. I'm sure something like that is in the sale contract. If it's destroyed, no one can ever prove anything. So Byrnes is home free. As am I, as his accomplice."

Flavia nodded slowly. "Very convincing," she commented. "But why were you the first person to suggest it was a fake?"

He paused over that one, and rubbed his chin. "Ah. I don't know. I'll have to think about that." He looked at her hopefully.

Flavia rubbed her eyes, ran her hands through her hair and yawned. "Ah, well. Enough for one night. Tell me the rest later. You'd be great as your own prosecutor. A pity the system doesn't allow for it. But you're right. You are a leading suspect." She stood up to let him out.

"And I can only think of one way for you to get off our list of potential Raphael roasters," she said as he went through the door.

"How's that?" he asked.

"Find us another one."

9

AT seven the next morning, Flavia walked into Bottando's office to see what was going on, and to arrange for the speedy interviewing of their suspects. As usual, she forgot to knock, and the General looked up at her angrily as she came in. Very unlike him.

"Tired and moody, are you?" she asked breezily.

He didn't reply, but handed over the last editions of the morning papers. Flavia glanced at them, and conceded inwardly that maybe he had a right to be moody. "Oh. Hadn't thought of that," she said apologetically.

"I had," he snapped. "But I didn't think it would be as bad as this."

She looked over them again. Until yesterday, Bottando's known fondness for food had always endeared him to the press. Now they laid into him with some violence, and in remarkable detail. In truth, he did look a little silly over the affair. Head of the art squad quaffing champagne and having a good time while mad arsonist destroys world's greatest masterpiece in the next room.

"You have to admit, it's got a funny side," she began, knowing it was the wrong thing to say.

"Flavia," said Bottando sternly.

"Yes, boss?"

"Shut up, dear."

"OK. Sorry."

He leaned back in his seat and sighed heavily. "It isn't funny at all," he said. "We don't have much time. Either we get someone soon, or the department will be massacred. We are caught," he observed acidly, "on the horns of a dilemma."

"Meaning that if you say it was a fake, Tommaso will tear you limb from limb, and if you don't, the press will?" Bottando nodded at her summary.

"Couldn't you just tell the minister, and get him to keep quiet?"

Bottando laughed. "A minister? Keep quiet? Contradiction in terms. I'd sooner take out a full-page advert in *il giornale*." He gestured vaguely at the most hostile of the newspapers. "No, I'm afraid we've no alternative. We'll just have to get results quickly. Besides, our case about Morneau is beginning to look a little feeble."

"Why's that?"

He handed over a sheet of paper. "Telegram from Janet. He screwed the log out of the Swiss."

Flavia looked at it with disappointment. Morneau's box had last been opened in August by someone else. They didn't know who. But it was well after the painting had been revealed to the public. "Damn it," she said. "Still, it doesn't mean that those sketches were put in then, though."

"No, but it weakens our case somewhat. That evidence is now very inconclusive. I'm sure it's also dawned on you that after last night we can't run any more tests on the picture to see if it really was genuine."

"You could always arrest someone. Last refuge of the incompetent, I know, but it would win us some time. Looks good for a few days, even if it's the wrong person."

"I was thinking about that. Maybe pulling in Argyll. Mad Englishman. Disappointed hopes. It would go down very well. The press think all Englishmen are lunatics."

Flavia looked worried: "Oh, no. Not Jonathan. That's not a very good idea."

Bottando regarded her dubiously. "Jonathan? Jonathan? What's this Jonathan bit?"

She disregarded the question. "If Byrnes didn't produce the real thing, that means that the genuine article is still out there. Somewhere, someone has a Raphael hanging on their wall, even if they don't know it."

"Argyll," she continued carefully, minding her words, "is probably our best chance of finding it. After all, if the thing exists, it's under a Mantini, and he's the only person who would know where to begin looking. If you lock him up he won't be able to help at all."

"True. But if the press finds out that we are relying on one of our prime suspects to help us in this, it'll make matters worse, not better."

She smiled at him. "That's easy enough. You don't need to have anything to do with him. I'll do that. I'm not in the force, so you can honestly say that the polizia has no contacts with this man. If anyone asks."

Bottando grunted. "All right. But he'll need watching carefully." He picked up a sheet of paper he'd been writing on earlier and gazed at it mournfully. "We have quite a lot of suspects to talk to today."

"Such as?"

"Anyone who might have known Morneau, which is, in theory, almost anyone in the art world. People who didn't like Tommaso, again everyone in the art world. People who wanted to be very rich. Again, everyone in the art world. Universal motive, universal opportunity."

"Except that whoever burnt the picture must have been at that party," she pointed out, sitting down and putting her feet on the low coffee table.

"That still leaves us with an embarrassing surfeit," he responded. "Dear me, what a mess. And if we don't get results pretty fast we're going to be roasted ourselves."

He looked round at her. "I suppose we'd better get going. So get your feet off my desk, damn you, and start dogging Argyll's steps."

• • •

"WE need to prove the picture was a forgery, which is difficult now it's destroyed. The notebooks help, but they're not conclusive. So we have to find the original original, so to speak."

Flavia was sitting in the kitchen of Argyll's new apartment. He'd explained when she knocked on the door that he'd taken up the offer by his old friend, Rudolf Beckett, of a spare room. He looked tired and told her that he had not, in the circumstances, slept very well. Flavia might have been more sympathetic had she not been so alarmed at the possibilities suggested by the fact that suspect number one was living in the same flat as a journalist.

Argyll, however, reassured her. His flatmate was at the moment in Sicily on an extended trip to write stories about the Mafia. Flavia wondered whether any reporter ever went to Sicily to do anything else. He would not be back for several days, at least, so she stopped worrying and got back to the subject of Argyll's chance to rehabilitate himself.

"If the evidence about the forgery is so weak, why are you convinced?"

Flavia held up her hand and counted off the points, one by one. "Firstly, I want to be, because I hate the idea of a genuine Raphael being charred. Secondly, because otherwise we're looking for a real nutcase, and I don't want to believe that either. Thirdly, because we've got to explore all the possibilities anyway. Fourthly, intuition. Fifthly, because I trust your judgement."

Argyll snorted. "Sixthly, you're also crazy. Certainly you're the only person who trusts my judgement. But I'm just a graduate student. I can't really see myself wandering around looking for picture forgers."

"Indeed not. But you know more about that damned man Mantini than anyone else. He's now very much the artistic flavour of the month. The end of our troubles probably lies somewhere in your file cards."

Argyll brushed his fingers through his hair, hummed a little, then twiddled his thumbs, all symptoms that Flavia now recognised as symptomatic of embarrassment on his part.

"Yes, lovely. Glad to oblige. But, I mean, I hardly like to raise the subject and all that, but, well . . ."

"Why should you bother when you could possibly find it yourself and make a fortune?"

"I wasn't going to put it quite like that . . ."

"But I got hold of your general line of thought, correct?"

"Suppose."

"Simple enough," she said sweetly. "Step more than a centimetre out of line and Bottando will arrest you as a prime suspect, and throw you to the wolves to get the press off his back. I had a very hard time this morning," she added with some exaggeration, "dissuading him from locking you up immediately. He found your reasoning about why he should very convincing. And, of course, if you are innocent, you would earn the immense gratitude of almost everyone from the prime minister down to myself, if you helped."

Argyll reached for another slice of toast, buttered it, and covered it with about a quarter inch of Beckett's expensively imported marmalade. "Oh, all right, then," he said grudgingly. "You have a persuasive way with you. But I must warn you that even my inestimable services don't guarantee success."

"There is your catalogue of Mantini's paintings."

"As yet incomplete. And that only deals with paintings that still exist. The number that must have been destroyed, or forgotten about, is probably huge."

"Do your best. We can talk about it this evening when you've thought about it. I must go off on my errands."

"One thing you can do for me. Could you use your contacts to ask around all the auction houses and dealers in order to trace any pictures that might have been bought by Morneau? And anyone else you might suspect?"

"Where?"

"All over Europe. Or at least the main centres."

"All over Europe for all our suspects? Is that all?"

He nodded. "I suppose it's a big task. But if you could find that one of them bought a picture the same size as that Raphael, it would help."

"I see. Anything else you want, by any chance?"

"Just tell me one thing. Do you think I had anything to do with this?"

Flavia picked up her bag and slung it over her shoulder,

brow furrowed for a moment as she weighed up the options of being truthful or of upsetting him with her lack of confidence in his honesty.

"Pass," she said eventually, and headed off before he could reply.

AFTER Flavia had run down the stairs in search of a taxi, Argyll wandered about his new apartment, tidying up in a halfhearted manner, wondering how best to go about his new task. It was hard to concentrate on the matter with the omnipresent thought that the slightest slip-up could land him in jail for much of the rest of his life. If he helped find the picture he might damn himself. But if he didn't, he would surely do so. It was not what had been in his mind when he thought of the pleasures of living in Rome once again. One thing was clear, however. He wasn't going to be able to confine himself to looking through file cards. He'd have to be a bit more active than that. Flavia, he thought, was basically well-disposed towards him, and disinclined to believe him responsible for all this. Her boss appeared to be of a different frame of mind.

Not that this one was going to be easy. He had never counted, but he reckoned that he had records of about five hundred pictures by Mantini. He knew that around half of these had been painted before 1724, before the painter covered over the Raphael. All the rest were either after that date or uncertain. He went to the shoe boxes of white cards which contained the records of the past three years' work and started flicking through. After a few minutes he decided that it would be easier simply to take cards out; putting them back in the right order could be taken care of later. Desperate situations require reckless remedies. About an hour's work produced a depressing result: even after the pictures which had been bought by the owner and stayed in the family's hands thereafter had been taken out, the pile of possibles was still about two inches thick—at about fifty cards to the inch.

Then he remembered Lady Arabella's letter, and went through again, removing everything but ruins and things that might get called ruins; this more than halved the problem to around forty-five pictures. He settled down, clamped his Walkman over his ears, put on a tape, and began to make a list. Not because it was especially vital, but because he couldn't think what to do next, and listening to music and making out lists he always found very therapeutic.

THE rest of the day passed in industrious boredom for all concerned. At the museum, Tommaso and his cohorts were doing their best to retrieve the situation, pumping out press releases. Bottando spent some of his time in similar pursuits, but eventually gave up what appeared to be a losing battle and turned his mind to more immediate tasks.

Clearly someone in the museum—and it had to be

Tommaso—was working furiously to shift the blame onto the police, Spello, and the ill-fated security council. He cursed the day he'd ever heard of that infernal committee. Not that he really blamed Tommaso, he thought in a fleeting moment of charitable objectivity, the man was trying to survive a calamity which had not been his fault. Perfectly understandable; it was simply that he wished the director wasn't trying to do so by offering Bottando's head as a substitute for his own. Perhaps Bottando would have done the same thing, in similar circumstances. Perhaps. But he was sure he would have been more tactful about it, and not tried to torpedo someone who, at the moment, was doing his damnedest to track down the real culprit.

His rivals in the various police forces were also well into a campaign against him, and he realised that the only effective answer to them was an arrest or two. So he dictated a bland statement about pursuing all possible investigations and being confident of making an arrest soon—which they could do, he thought gloomily. It was just that they would have no idea whether they'd collared the right man.

Then he deployed his forces to interview the partygoers, and himself went over to the National Museum to brief the director, as well as to talk to the man's principal enemies. Not all of them. There weren't enough hours in the day.

The briefing was tense, with Tommaso feigning concerned affability and Bottando pretending he hadn't noticed anything, so it was with considerable relief that he turned to the miscellaneous witnesses and suspects, whom he suspected would be more agreeable company. He started with Manzoni, summoning him to Ferraro's office, which he'd taken over for the duration. The restorer came in, moving uneasily and looking like a wreck. Bottando wasn't certain whether it was from emotional distress about the picture or the after-effects of his drinking the night before. He didn't ask.

The questioning, on the whole, was routine. Where was he, who did he talk to, and so on. All accounted for up to the moment when he had wandered away from Bottando. "And then?"

"To be perfectly frank, I can't remember. I haven't the faintest idea who I talked to. I remember lecturing someone about the restoration of prints. I know that, because I thought to myself that, if I'd been sober, I'd realise I was being extraordinarily dull."

Bottando considered this and then, with apparent indifference, started off on another tack. "Tell me," he said, "were you one of the people who did the tests on that picture? I looked through the report the other day. You signed it, didn't you?"

Manzoni nodded. "I did. I was in charge of the operation. The actual tests were carried out by the English experts called in by Byrnes who were more familiar with the machinery."

"I see. So Byrnes's people actually had their hands on the painting?" The man nodded.

"And you were entirely satisfied?"

"Of course," he said a little primly. The question had evidently pricked at his pride. "If I hadn't been I would have said so. They were men of the highest reputation. The picture passed every test with room to spare. I didn't have a shred of doubt." He stopped and bit his thumbnail thoughtfully, then looked up. "At least I didn't until about thirty seconds ago."

"What do you mean?" asked Bottando uncomfortably, conscious of a certain lack of subtlety in his interviewing technique.

"Not all technicians are idiots, you know," the man continued, the slightly priggish air growing, rather than fading in strength as he spoke.

"Tommaso's reputation rested on that Raphael. But if there's something wrong with it, Tommaso's credit-rating falls and Spello will get the job. It was burnt either as a way of getting at him or for some other motive. You, for no apparent reason, are spending some time reading the technical reports when presumably you have more urgent things to worry about. Which leads me to suspect . . ."

"Which leads you to suspect nothing whatsoever. But you've got a good imagination." Bottando hurriedly got up to end the interview, feeling slightly alarmed at the way the conversation had run away from him. Hung over or not, that young man had forged connections far too fast. He didn't like it.

He accompanied the restorer to the door, showing him out into the small anteroom that was normally occupied by the secretary. His next candidate sat there, placidly waiting.

"I see you're going to have a busy day," Manzoni said by way of farewell, "but I'd like to talk to you again, if you don't mind. If you want I'll go through the report again and see if there were any holes."

"Could there be any?"

"I'd rather read it again first, to make sure of my facts. And give it a bit of quiet thought. Besides, I don't want to disrupt your schedule. Maybe I could come round to your office after work to give you my impressions? About seven this evening?"

Bottando agreed, watched him go, then turned to ask Spello to come in. One down, eighty to go, he thought. Maybe Flavia can help out this afternoon. He watched the Etruscan specialist sit himself cautiously into the chair, and considered how best to start the questioning.

He needn't have bothered. Spello began on his own, with a forthright statement of fact. "You're talking to me because I'm one of your more promising arsonists," he stated. "Jilted out of my rightful job as the next director by Tommaso's machinations."

"So, burned up inside, you took your revenge by burning up his prize picture?"

Spello smiled. "And thus, at a stroke, creating a scandal, wrecking Tommaso's power to recommend anyone and assuring myself of the job. Easily done, especially as you'd already told me it was a fake, so there was no harm done. No. I did nothing of the sort, but I admit it's a convincing hypothesis."

"Except, of course, that our main evidence of faking has been considerably weakened. The painting may well have been genuine."

The man blanched visibly at the statement. Why was that? Simple objective distress at the loss? Bottando felt intensely awkward. Spello seemed positively eager to explain why he should be arrested immediately.

"Were you ever alone yesterday evening? Could you have slipped off without anyone noticing?"

"Nothing simpler. I hate those gatherings. I have to turn up, but I find the heat, the conversation and the company oppressive. I normally sneak off and go and read a book or something to recover myself, then go back again. I was up here for about an hour yesterday evening. All on my own. No one saw me come, no one saw me go."

How distressingly honest. If he'd wanted to make life easy for the police, he should either have come up with a cast-iron alibi, or with one that could be undermined. Candidly admitting he had none at all made everything very much more difficult.

"When I told you about the possible forgery, you kept it to yourself," Bottando began, swinging on to a new line. He was not happy. So far his performance at these interviews, where he was meant to be so masterfully in charge, was not at all good. He had lost the upper hand with the restorer, and seemed to be repeating the process with Spello. Perhaps the pressure was beginning to tell on him.

"If you'd really been after the directorship you would have started spreading rumours, surely?"

Spello shook his head. "Not necessarily," he said in a reasonable and distant tone. "Firstly, it could have been traced back to me. Secondly, without proof, Tommaso could brazen it out and put the rumours down to a smear campaign by the discontented—which it would have been. I'm still very doubtful. No matter what Manzoni thinks, I doubt he'll be able to punch a hole in those tests."

Bottando grunted, and tried again. "The fire alarm," he pointed out. "How did you do that?" He noticed that he'd stopped using the hypothetical language of conditional clauses. Spello noticed it as well, and for the first time the policeman saw a flicker of unease on the old man's face.

"*If* I did," he replied with emphasis, "I did what was actually done. Removed the perfectly good fuse, and replaced it with one that was burnt out. Thus, it would seem as though the fuse blew at random."

Bottando sat up in his seat. "How do you know that's what happened?" he asked.

"I talked to the electrician. He's an old fogey like me. Been here for years, like me. We've always got on well. He was a bit upset when he saw the fuse. Said he was sure he'd changed it over and put a new one in. Not at all like the well-used one found in the slot. I thought it was obvious; they'd been swapped. Chances were that no one would notice, or draw any conclusions if they did."

Bottando sat silently, thinking it over. Spello's account made perfectly good sense, and at least solved one problem of how it was done. It also tended to swing suspicion more firmly on Spello. Who realised it.

"So you see. Motive, opportunity and no alibi. Enough to arrest me on, if that's what you feel like doing."

"Yes," he agreed, then went on more formally. "For the time being, however, we're not arresting anyone. But I must warn you not to leave Rome for the next few days. Any attempt to do so will be treated as attempted flight. Do you understand?"

"Perfectly, General," came the equally stiff reply, which then turned into a conspiratorial smile. "But I can tell you that if you do arrest me, you'll be making a big mistake. It'll be all Tommaso needs to restore his reputation. Because of that committee, you'll go down with me."

10

IT was seven-thirty in the evening. Bottando sat in his office, waiting for Manzoni to show up. He wanted to see the man, especially since Manzoni had rung up in the early afternoon to say that he had found something which might be of interest. But the restorer was late. Often the case with these sort of people, but Bottando, who still retained some vague elements of his earlier military training, was irritated nonetheless. Punctuality, he thought, was a very great virtue; not that so many of his countrymen agreed with him. He filled the time catching up on some work and trying to control his mounting ill-humour.

While he was muttering about lack of consideration and the indignity of full generals being made to wait by junior restorers, Flavia had arrived at Argyll's flat to see what progress he'd made during his day's work. There was no answer. Despite her express request that he be there, he'd gone out. Damn him. She thought for a moment that maybe the bell didn't work. It was an old, run-down block and that was a distinct possibility. So she went into a bar and telephoned. Still no answer.

She was furious, and starting thinking along the lines that were currently occupying her boss back in the office. She'd had a tiring day and was frustrated at having worked so hard for almost no result. And to be stood up by someone who was lucky not to be in jail already was outrageous.

The high point, or low point, of her day's business had been a visit to Sir Edward Byrnes. Unlike Bottando, she had not been faced with a virtual confession, and she'd found it difficult to ask all the questions she needed without bringing up their suspicions about the origins of the picture.

Byrnes had to believe that all they were after was the person with the wandering aerosol. There was no need to show all their cards, especially as, in her book, the successful and wealthy Englishman was far and away the most likely suspect.

She found him in his hotel: it was highly expensive and, typically, not one of the more obviously opulent affairs that are to be found around the via Veneto. Rather, Byrnes's combination of money and exquisite taste had landed him in a highly anonymous but very private and splendidly elegant palazzo off the Corso, where the few guests allowed in reposed as though they were at home with the servants.

In the delicate pink-and-white drawing room, deserted apart from the two of them, Byrnes sat Flavia down on a sofa, arranged himself opposite her in a tapestry-covered armchair, and summoned a waiter with a brief wave of his hand. He was at their side in a commendably respectful matter of seconds.

"A drink, Signorina?" he asked in flawless Italian. "Or are you going to say 'not while I'm on duty,' eh?" He blinked in an amiably owlish fashion from behind thick pebble-like glasses as he spoke. There were two ways of interpreting that, Flavia decided. On the one hand, it might be a good-natured look that goes along with someone trying to make himself agreeable. On the other, it might be an expression of contentment from someone who knows he's got away with it.

"Not me, Sir Edward. I think that's only for the English police. Besides, I'm not in the police."

"Good. Very sensible." She wasn't sure what part of her reply he referred to. He ordered two glasses of champagne kir without asking her opinion on the matter. "Now, how can I help you?"

Not, thought Flavia, "What do you want?" He's keen to sound more accommodating than that. Doesn't mean he will be any more forthcoming, mind you.

Flavia smiled at him. He was ordinarily not someone who let anybody do the talking, let alone a woman. "Obviously it's about the Raphael, and the events of yesterday . . ."

"And you want to know whether I habitually go around with aerosols of gasoline in my pocket? Or if I saw anyone looking especially furtive?"

"Something like that. Routine questioning of everyone in the museum yesterday evening, you understand."

"Especially if they happened to be responsible for the picture being there in the first place," he observed, taking out a short stubby pipe and beginning to fill it from a leather pouch. The trouble with everybody in this business is that they're too quick on the uptake, she thought.

"I wish I could provide you with some helpful comment. I am, of course, deeply upset by the whole thing. I'd formed a great attachment to the picture, and was very proud of my role in it. I gather it's beyond repair?"

If Byrnes hadn't been responsible for burning the picture, he would, naturally, want to know how successful the attack had been. Flavia nodded, and he nodded back in acknowledgement. He was still filling the pipe, which was evidently a highly complex and technical operation. His head was bent over as he shovelled a remarkable amount of tobacco into the bowl, then tamped it into place with a little metal device apparently designed for just such a purpose. While he was doing this, with immense concentration, she couldn't see his face at all well. Eventually he looked up at her again, stuck the pipe in his mouth and continued, not having noticed the long break in the conversation.

"You get fond of them, when you're with them for a long time," he said absently. "Especially this one. I watched over it very carefully, once I realised what it was. The high point of my career. And now this. It was an appalling thing to happen. From what I've read, it would have been difficult to prevent as well. You seem to be looking for a madman, and it's impossible to guard against random acts." He now began on the equally intricate business of turning the pipe bowl into a minor inferno. Smoke billowed out in profusion, and drifted in a thick smog across the room.

"I'm sure you understand that we have to establish everybody's whereabouts for the entire evening?" Flavia said, tearing her eyes away from the pipe and getting back to business.

"Of course. That's simple. I arrived at the hotel at about six, checked in and walked straight to the museum. I talked to various people and was still there when the announcement about the, ah, incident was made at about eight." He reeled off a list of names. She jotted them down.

"And how long did you spend talking to each of these people? With Argyll, for instance," she said casually. He didn't appear to make any connection of significance.

"With him longer than most, I suppose. As he may have told you already, I'm financing his trip here, and I quite like talking to him."

She nodded. "May I ask why you gave him this money?"

"Mild guilt. Or rather sympathy. Or is it empathy? I heard afterwards that he, like the person who commissioned me, was on the trail of this picture, but that I got there faster. That often happens, of course, and I've been pipped at the post myself. Ordinarily I just see it as the luck of the game. Except that it was such a big prize and Argyll was clearly counting on it for his work, rather than for simple financial profit. So I thought that the least I could do would be to offer some form of recompense. He does, in fact, deserve it. His work is much better than he makes out. A little sloppy over details . . ."

That's true, thought Flavia to herself.

". . . but essentially well-researched and interesting. Not nearly as narrow as the subject suggests. So I'm not giving favours to the undeserving poor," he concluded.

"So you noticed nothing at this party and were never on your own?"

"Only when Argyll disappeared off to the toilet, or to get some drinks, or something like that. He was quite flustered all evening. I think he was excited at being back in Rome."

Well, maybe so. She switched the subject once more. "You talk about being commissioned?" she prompted.

"My little secret," he replied. "Most of my colleagues and rivals still believe I owned the picture. I let them think it because it drives them into such paroxysms of jealousy. All I did was act as an agent. I shipped it back, sent it to the restorers and organised the sale."

"Why did you choose these particular people?"

"No reason. They were available, I'd worked with them before and knew them to be reliable. They were very excited. They were in the office from the moment the crate arrived: we could hardly keep them away from it."

"Could you give me their names?"

"By all means. I'm sure they would be pleased to talk to you. One of them rang me this morning, very upset indeed. They became very proprietorial about it—always saying how lucky I was to own such a picture. I couldn't bear to disillusion them."

"Who did it belong to then?" Flavia leant forward in her chair in anticipation. He might lie. Almost certainly would. But even so it might provide something to go on. Even if it turned out to be a lie, his assertion would prove something.

Byrnes spread his hands over the desk. "I wish I knew. I was given instructions by letter from a lawyer in Luxembourg. It was a bit odd, I know, but such procedures are not entirely unknown. There is often a certain amount of disguise when some rich family wants to raise some cash discreetly. To buy and sell a picture anonymously is more unusual, but at the time I thought the picture was not especially valuable. So I could see no reason for not going ahead."

"But you weren't tempted to keep the picture when you knew what it was?"

Byrnes smiled at her. "It occurred to me, of course. But by that time I'd signed a contract as the agent. Besides, it's not the way I operate. As you know, the art-dealing community is not noted for its impeccable integrity,"—here Flavia grinned—"but there is a sort of honour among thieves, and not pinching someone else's discovery is part of it. That's why I felt a little guilty about Argyll.

"But quite apart from the moral issue, I didn't know who was behind it all. For all I know, it might have been the Vatican itself. It always needs ready money these days, and this method might have been a way of circumventing the objections to the sale which would otherwise have developed. It never does to offend someone if you don't know who you are offending. Besides, the retainer alone was very generous."

"You were never suspicious that something might be wrong?" Flavia asked doubtfully.

"Of course. I haven't worked in the art business for a quarter of a century without learning to trust no one. But I chose the people who tested it. They were in no doubt that it was genuine, nor was the Museo Nazionale. I could see nothing wrong. If I'd had the slightest doubt, I'd never have agreed to the museum's terms in the sale contract."

"Which were?"

"Simply that if the painting's authenticity was called into question I'd be responsible for refunding the money as agent for the owner. Very tight and carefully drafted. They included it, I suppose, to satisfy the finance ministry that they were being careful with the taxpayer's money. Besides, Tommaso was involved and we've never got on, even though we keep up an appearance of friendliness."

Flavia said nothing in reply to this, but sat quietly, waiting to see if he would continue on his own. In a fit of what was either calculating revelation, or confessional zeal, he did so.

"You see, I once sold Tommaso a Correggio. Doubts were cast on its authenticity, and Tommaso threatened me, saying that if I didn't take it back, I'd never sell another picture in Italy. There was nothing in the contract which said I had to. But I did, out of a sense of pride. Nonetheless, he still made life as difficult for me as possible for the next fifteen years. So it was quite a triumph to get him to take that Raphael, even if the terms were stiff. He hated doing it, but his desire for the picture was too great."

He shrugged as a way of showing his bewilderment with the ways of God and men. "Ah well. That's all past history now. The terms of that contract seem to be redundant. The painting's destroyed." He smiled gently at her. "So there's nothing for me to take back even if they wanted me to, is there?"

THAT, essentially, had been the interesting part of the day; the rest was spent listening to people explain how—and why—they hadn't seen anything interesting or significant at the party. Out of more than eighty people, some sixty-five, Flavia reckoned, could easily have slipped out of the room unnoticed, gone upstairs, set light to the picture and come back down again. Of that sixty-five, around fifty knew about the alarm system. Of the remaining fifteen, nearly all could easily have found out.

More frustrating and personally irritating was the fact that she found herself quite liking Byrnes and being seduced—well, perhaps seduced was not the right word—by his charm. She'd gone in to see him determined to be distant, cold and efficient, but despite these laudable intentions, she found herself enjoying talking to him, and warming to his odd combination of vagueness and business acumen.

And the man had taken advantage of the fact. As she was leaving, he'd casually mentioned he was going back to London that evening, and would he be required for the investigation any more? Damn right, he would; but she could find no pretext upon which to detain him. He was evidently intent on going and they could not require him to stay without announcing that he was a suspect. But on what grounds if she couldn't mention the forgery? Equally, by politely asking permission to leave, he had countered any suggestion that he was hotfooting it to safety.

All she could do was lamely say that, of course, it was quite in order for him to go. He'd spent some time laying out his motives for destroying the picture—revenge, greed, the works—and all she could do at the end was wish him a safe trip home. He'd thanked her soberly, and wished her luck in the investigation. Was he laughing at her? Surely he was, but that poker face, moderated by thick glasses and clouds of smoke, had been impenetrable.

Then there had been the interminable interviews, often tramping over ground that—she found to her irritation—had already been worked over by Bottando, and, on top of that, her ears ringing and her head spinning, her useless visit to Argyll's apartment. At quarter to eight, tired, weary and wanting only to go home and have a bath and an early night, she dragged herself up the stairs of the office to write up a few reports. This made her feel virtuous, but did nothing else to cheer her up at all. She had a feeling that disaster was just around the corner.

She was wrong, as she often seemed to be these days: it was lumbering down the stairs, in the shape of a perspiring, out of breath and evidently troubled Bottando.

"Flavia. Good. Come with me," was all he said as he hurried past her. She turned round and followed him to his car in the square. Clearly it was serious; it took more than a small crisis to break the General out of his habitual slow amble. They both got in the back, Bottando gave the driver an address in Trastevere, and told him to hurry. He did so, complete with sirens, horn and screeching tyres for dramatic effect.

"What's happened now?" she asked as she regained her balance after a particularly vicious corner.

"I told you about Manzoni, the restorer?" She nodded. "He was meant to come and see me at seven. He didn't show up. The Trastevere police just rang: he didn't come because he was dead. It seems that someone has murdered him."

Flavia sat stunned. Things were going from bad to worse. "Are they sure it was murder?"

"Knife in the back," he replied simply.

"Oh dear," she said. Complications, nothing but complications. It wouldn't make Bottando look any better to have a witness murdered under his nose. It made solving the case more difficult, and now there was a murder mixed up in it all, there would be demarcation disputes with the murder squad and others, as they squabbled over who should be in charge. The investigation could disintegrate into one of those well-known Italian situations where everybody spends their time fighting their colleagues, and nothing whatsoever gets done. She'd seen it before. The General was evidently thinking along the same lines.

"Listen," he said as the car drew up at their destination. "Leave the talking to me here. Don't say anything more than you need to, all right?"

Following behind him at a distance suitable for a junior tagging along, therefore, she climbed the stairs and entered Manzoni's apartment. It was full of policemen, photographers, fingerprint men, neighbours and people just hanging around. The usual chaos. Bottando was spotted by the senior local detective, who came over and introduced himself.

"When we discovered he worked at the museum I decided it might have something to do with you, so I called," he explained after relating how the body had been discovered by a neighbour peering in through the open front door as she passed.

Bottando shrugged and walked over to the body, ignoring the invitation to talk. "Any idea when he was killed?"

"After five-thirty, when he was seen coming home, and before seven, when the body was discovered. So far we can't be more precise than that. Right-hand blow to the back and into the heart. Kitchen knife."

"No one saw any strangers hanging about, I suppose?"

The detective shook his head. "Any idea what it may be about?"

Bottando pursed his lips and shook his head slowly. "No," he lied. "My first inclination is to suggest coincidence, much as I dislike them. He certainly wasn't a hot tip for our arsonist. Nor was there any connection I know of between him and any of our suspects."

The detective looked disgruntled. He knew Bottando was being elusive, but in the very hierarchical police force, there is no way you can press a general without running the risk of getting yourself into trouble. He would have to find someone of equivalent rank to do that for him.

While the little interchange was going on, and while her boss wandered around the apartment looking vainly for hints, Flavia leant on the small round table in the sitting-room and pursued her own thoughts. They didn't lead anywhere, except to the depressing conclusion that while they had had two crimes and too many suspects this morning; now they had three crimes and too many suspects. Not her idea of progress.

She told Bottando this after they left the apartment. He

dismissed the car, explaining that walking helped him think. Besides, it was one of the few things he found pleasant at the moment. She fell in step with him and talked. He marched morosely by her side, not saying a word in reply for several minutes.

"So what you're basically saying is that we're no further on at all? And in fact we're more confused than ever?" he said when her exposition was finished.

"Well, yes, I suppose I am. But we could try and narrow it down a little." Bottando grunted, but kept quiet. Flavia was wearing baggy trousers and a jacket, and now thrust her hands into the pockets to help her concentrate. They crossed the Tiber as the dusk was deepening into dark. A thin but chilly wind was coming up the river, making her shiver as they walked.

"OK then," she began after a few moments. "Either the picture was a forgery or it wasn't. If it wasn't, then we must look for a madman or someone in the museum. Correct?" It was a rhetorical question. Even had it not been it probably wouldn't have got a reply from her companion, who was staring moodily at the pavement.

"Main candidates, Manzoni, deceased, and Spello. Both disliking Tommaso, prompted into desperate action by the announcement of his retirement."

"Who killed Manzoni?"

"Spello," she said firmly. "Realised Manzoni had wrecked the painting. Overcome with rage that he'd destroyed such a beautiful object. Or realised Manzoni knew *he'd* burnt the picture, so killed him to shut him up."

"This is narrowing it down, is it?"

Flavia ploughed on, ignoring the interruption. "Other candidate: Argyll, overcome with remorse at his lost opportunity . . ."

She got no further in what she considered a masterly exposition of the options. "Flavia, dear, this is not cheering me up. Do you, in fact, have the slightest idea who might be responsible for this?"

"Well, um, no."

"I thought not. Now, why the timing?"

"What do you mean?"

"I mean, why was the picture burnt yesterday? After all, we'd just come across the evidence it was a fake and hadn't told anyone. And the evidence, it seems, wasn't as good as we thought. So why destroy it?"

This one stumped her, so he carried on on his own. "I think," he pointed out, mentally counting, "you have just listed about a dozen combinations of possibilities, without a shred of real evidence for any of them. Which goes to show that armchair detection is no good for anything. We need evidence of something. I reckon it's about time you stopped thinking and started looking."

"Where do you suggest?"

"Go to London. Manzoni seems to have come up with something, and we need to know what it was. If those tests have a hole, the only place you'll find out is there. Go and see those restorers. That might provide something. Could you get on a plane tomorrow?"

She nodded. "As long as someone can keep an eye on

Argyll while I'm away," she said. "Perhaps," she added, "I should nip off now and see if he's back in. You never know, he might open the door covered in blood."

"And might stick a knife in you for good measure."

"I can't see him doing something like that. But I can't see any of them doing anything like that. That's the trouble."

"Don't let your intuition run away with you. If it wasn't for the timing of all this, he'd be charged already. So watch yourself. Unless he comes up with a very good reason for what he's been up to, let me know and I'll pull him in.

"I feel uncomfortable about all this," he continued. "I'm missing something which should be obvious. Something a long time ago which isn't right. I woke up this morning and almost had it, but it slipped away. It's driving me quietly crazy. Having an impossible task is bad enough, but when you suspect it's because of your own failing memory it becomes insufferable."

They parted at the next corner, Bottando walking northwards, slowly, absent-mindedly and morosely; she with the brisk step of a person who cannot remain bothered and overburdened for too long.

ARGYLL was at home this time, let her in, and burbled happily about his day for the first few minutes, not letting Flavia get a word in edgeways. She sat quietly and waited for him to stop.

"There's nothing like the prospect of spending the rest of your life in jail to make you get a move on," he said. "I reckon if my supervisor had threatened to send me to Wormwood Scrubs for a year or two, I could have had my thesis finished ages ago."

He gestured over to a desk piled high with files, file-cards, used coffee cups and stacks of paper. "See that? I've been working like a demon all day."

"All day?" she asked quietly.

"Yup. Non-stop. Quite possessed I was. I've got it down to about twenty possibles. Assuming, that is, that it exists at all. But if I didn't assume that, I'd lose heart. With a bit of luck I'll be off your list of potential jail fodder within a week or so."

"All day?" she repeated. "What about when I came round at seven?"

He paused. "Oh. I'd forgotten all about that. That's what comes of concentrating. You were meant to come round, weren't you?"

She nodded. "And I did. At seven. And you weren't here."

"Yes I was. I'd just forgotten all about it. I had my Walkman on, so I suppose I didn't hear the bell."

"Was anyone else here? Can anyone give you an alibi?"

Argyll looked flustered. "An alibi? For heaven's sake! Of course not. I was here all on my own. I know it was careless of me. I'm sorry. But is it really such a big thing?"

"Yes," she said. And explained why. The colour drained from his cheeks as she spoke.

"So you think I slipped out, knifed him, came home and pretended I'd been here all the time, not hearing you because of the music?"

"Fits the facts, doesn't it?"

"Rather well," he agreed unhappily. "Except, of course, that it's not at all what I was doing. I was here."

He rummaged around in Beckett's drinks cupboard, pulled out a bottle of grappa and poured a healthy glassful. "I don't suppose he'd object in the circumstances." He took a heavy suck on the glass, coughed slightly, then offered her a drink herself. She declined.

"I suppose," he restarted with some hesitation, ferociously scratching the top of his head in a way that indicated profound misgivings inside, "I suppose that what I was planning to do next will make things worse."

He stopped, and she gazed at him enquiringly. "I was about to tell you," he went on, "that to finish the search for this picture I would have to go to look at some things in London. I was thinking of going tomorrow."

He looked at her hopefully. "Remarkable timing," she said sarcastically. "Especially considering that Byrnes headed off for England this evening as well."

It was not the reassurance that Argyll had been looking for. Indeed, it made him even less comfortable. The drink rested on the floor, completely forgotten.

"So it would look better if I stayed here?"

"It would look better. But practically speaking, I suppose, it might be better if you went. As long as I go with you and you tell me exactly where you'll be at every moment of the day. One more slip and I'll pull you in. And I mean that. Depending on what turns up, I might do it anyway. Agreed?"

He nodded. "I suppose so. I'm grateful for your trust in me."

"Don't be sarcastic. And I don't trust you. Except, of course, that I find it difficult to believe that anyone could have forged a picture like that and act as dimwittedly as you have. At the moment the only thing you've got going for you is stupidity. You're very lucky not to be in a cell already."

So, sometimes you say the wrong thing. Flavia could, at times, be a little harsh in her conversational gambits, and the characteristic tended to show itself when she was tired or frustrated. This evening she was both of these, and worried as well. The combination eroded the natural kindness which generally masked her occasional tinge of verbal brutality.

Argyll, however, disregarded these extenuating circumstances and exploded.

"I think we ought to get one thing clear here," he began coldly. "I never said that picture was a Raphael, I simply came out to Rome to check. I went by the rulebook, not making claims I couldn't substantiate or prove. Whatever happened thereafter was nothing to do with me. So remember that. Secondly, it was me, not you, who first suggested it might be a fake. If it wasn't for my research, which you sneer at so much, you'd be running around wringing your hands at the loss of a masterpiece. Thirdly, you don't have any evidence against me at all. If you had, you'd have locked me up already. So don't imply you're doing me any favours.

"And finally, at the moment, you need my help more than I need yours. If you think you can find that picture on your own, go ahead. But you can't. I can, maybe. And I'm not going to help you if I'm going to be subjected to sneering little taunts from you all the time. Is that clear?"

On the whole, it was not a bad speech at all. Later on, lying in bed, thinking about it and making little improvements for the benefit of posterity, he was struck by his simple eloquence. Forceful, no-nonsense stuff, in fact. He was quite pleased with himself. Opportunities for righteous indignation come up only very infrequently, and he normally never thought of the appropriately devastating response until, on average, about forty-five minutes afterwards.

More satisfying still, it stopped the voluble Italian woman dead in her tracks. He was ordinarily very mild-mannered; his expressions of rage were most visibly expressed in a faint look of distress or a mumbled sentence of mild disapproval. Oratory was quite out of character and the suddenness of the speech, combined with the real feeling that apparently went into it, momentarily caught Flavia unawares. She stared at him in surprise, dismissed the temptation to fire back a full broadside, then apologised.

"I'm sorry. It's been a bad day. Truce? No more comments until you're cleared?"

He stumped around the room, closed the curtains, shut a cupboard door or two while he worked off his indignation, then nodded. "Or arrested, I suppose," he added. "OK. A deal. When do we leave?"

"There's a plane at seven-thirty. I shall pick you up here at six-thirty."

"That early? How horrible."

"Get used to it," she said as she got ready to leave. "In Italian prisons they wake you up at five . . . Sorry," she added quickly. "Shouldn't have said that."

11

NOT to be outworked by his assistant, Bottando was sitting down at his desk, the inevitable coffee before him, around the same time that Flavia and Argyll were boarding the plane for London. In the cold light of dawn, he was less than convinced that letting either of them go was a good idea.

But he'd allowed himself to be persuaded by her arguments. Which were, essentially, that as things stood they had no real evidence of anything at all; that if Argyll was guilty he had to be allowed to make some mistake, and if he was innocent he had to find that picture, or prove that it didn't exist and the one in the museum had been genuine. Besides which, as she somewhat tactlessly pointed out, they'd made so many mistakes so far in this business, one more would hardly make any great difference.

The comment accented the still ferocious assaults in the newspapers that lay before him. They had discovered about Manzoni, and were painting lurid pictures about what they had now dubbed the "museum of murder." Tommaso had been no friendlier when he'd told him of the latest developments. He'd been clearly upset about the restorer's demise, no doubt concluding that, if this whole thing was a plot against him, then he might be next in line for a knife in the back.

Bottando had misjudged that man, it was clear. In the immediate aftermath of the party, the director had presented a humble, subdued, almost likeable side, though this was evidently an uncharacteristic reaction brought on by shock, because it wasn't lasting. Tommaso was now getting very nervous, tense and short-tempered; not that such a condition stopped the politician in him operating at full power. He was manoeuvring with all the grace of a synchronised swimmer, rapidly and successfully shifting all blame on to the committee, Spello, and Bottando's department. Already stories hinting something along those lines had appeared in one of the papers.

One thing was certain. Bottando felt himself getting too old for this sort of thing. Wearily, he counted up the forces and assessed his chances. On his side, he had the ministry of defence, who could be counted on to look after him. He thought. Against him, he had the newspapers, the arts ministry, the interior ministry, and Tommaso. The treasury represented a floating vote, whose mind would be made up by the chances of getting its money back.

If they ever got that far. According to the legal department in the arts ministry, the contract stated clearly that if the picture was a fake, the seller—that is Edward Byrnes—would have to refund. Any loss of a genuine picture would be borne by the state. If Byrnes was telling the truth, if he hadn't owned the picture and didn't have the money, he'd still have to refund. But, as the man had told Flavia, the picture was gone. So the only way of proving it was a fake was to find the original.

Essentially, it came down to the fact that the future of his department and of his career now depended on a foreign graduate student, who had already made one mistake and who might very well be an arsonist, forger, conspirator, murderer, and half-cracked as well. The thought did not bolster the General's confidence. He was starting to suspect that, at long last and after many campaigns, he was outnumbered, outflanked and outgeneralled.

And Bottando's sense that he was missing something still nagged away at him. He'd paced the streets, sat in armchairs, tossed and turned in bed. All to no avail. He *was* missing something and was no nearer to discovering what it was. The more he tried, the more the wisp of memory receded. Hence the vast piles of dossiers on his desk. The personnel files of everyone in the museum, combined with what they knew about Morneau, Byrnes, Argyll, and anyone else concerned.

He picked up Tommaso's file. Might as well start at the top, he thought as he opened it. Cavaliere Marco Ottavio Mario di Bruno di Tommaso. Born March 3, 1938. Father, Giorgio Tommaso, died 1948, aged forty-two. Mother, Elena Maria Marco, died 1959, age fifty-seven. He jotted idly on his notepad and sighed heavily.

Pages and pages of the stuff, a monument to the excessive zeal of an overstocked bureaucracy with nothing better to do. Education, careers, opinions, recommendations. All repeated hundreds of times in each dossier on everyone. And he was going to go through the lot of them, for the one piece of information that might jog his memory.

BOTTANDO had polished off the Renaissance department when the plane touched down, and was progressing on to Early Medieval Painting by the time the taxi drew up outside the Victoria & Albert Museum to let Argyll out.

As agreed, he gave her a detailed itinerary; a couple of hours there, followed by a brief stop at the Courtauld in Portman Square, with an option on a visit to the British Museum later on. She told him to meet her at six, and concluded with dire warnings of the potential penalties should he miss the rendezvous again. He grinned nervously at her and made his way up the steps.

He had always hated the V & A, especially the library, which was his present destination. It was not just the fact that it was cold; nearly all libraries he had worked in were underheated. Nor was it particularly the clear evidence of a chronic lack of funds: the little donation boxes hopefully primed with five-pound notes to give visitors the right idea; the lack of proper lighting; the general air of woebegone neglect.

But in he went, walking through the museum along the echoing corridors, resisting the temptation to buy an overpriced bun in the café, up the stairs and into the library. For the next ten minutes he rummaged around in the catalogues, occasionally scribbling call numbers on bits of paper and handing them in at the desk. Then he gave in to temptation, took his newspaper and went down for a coffee. Long experience had taught him that no books would turn up for at least forty-five minutes.

Feeling oppressed and out of place, he took his coffee and soggy doughnut and sat in a far corner of the room, away from the other students and the small number of miscellaneous tourists. He concentrated on the paper and pretended, as best as he could, that he was somewhere else. His thoughts on the subject were interrupted by a clattering of plates as someone sat down at his table. The newcomer instantly fished out a packet of Rothman's from the pocket of his old, battered jacket—which had clearly once been the top half of a suit—and lit up.

"Thank heavens for that. First today. I've almost been chewing my fingers off up there."

"Hello, Phil. How are you?"

The newcomer shrugged. "As ever," he replied. He puffed furiously on his cigarette. He was one of Argyll's oldest associates. As Philip Mortimer-Jones, he was a child of privilege, public schools, and superlative contacts through his father, who was some big wheel in the National Trust. As plain Phil, he was short and stocky, abominably dressed, with dark greasy hair and a look on his face which made you suspect he was about to fall asleep, or that his eyes were caked with grime, or that he had just eaten some substance of which the police would disapprove: in all the five years he had known him, Argyll could never decide. Possibly all of the above. But for all his dormouse-like appearance Phil was a bright lad. He was also more finely tuned into the nuances of academic gossip than anyone else Argyll knew. He confirmed this with his next statement.

"Surprised to see you here. I thought you'd still be mourning over your great Italian disappointment."

Argyll groaned. If Phil knew then everybody would know. "Who told you about that?"

"Can't remember. Heard it somewhere."

How *did* he know, though? Argyll was certain he had told only one person, and that had been his ever-so-civil and discreet supervisor. It had been an awkward meeting, because his idleness had finally caught up with him. His university had become somewhat impatient and had threatened to wipe his name off the books. His supervisor, old Tramerton, had been asked for a recommendation one way or another, and he had asked Argyll for evidence that any sort of mental activity was still flickering.

He'd had to produce something convincing quickly. So in the space of four days he had gathered the only material to hand, accumulated an impressive-looking bibliography and posted off to Italy his tentative conclusion that underneath the Mantini rested a genuine, lost Raphael.

It seemed now, of course, that it was the wrong conclusion, but he refused to take responsibility for that. If the university authorities had not been so unreasonably demanding, the little paper would not have been written and Byrnes would not have got to the picture before him. Quite a pleasant chain of events, if you thought about it. Anyway, Tramerton had been convinced—of his efforts if not his scholarly merits—and had done the decent thing. The threat of execution was withdrawn and Argyll had thought no more about it.

Until now. Evidently either Tramerton had given the paper to someone or had told someone about it. Find who it was and the route to Byrnes would open up like magic. But who? His supervisor had been out of circulation in Italy, staying at a colleague's house west of Montepulciano, so a letter had said. How had Byrnes got at him there? He'd write and ask. Maybe that would produce something useful.

It would all have to wait for the time being; the aromatic confines of the library awaited him. He stopped his colleague just as he was getting into conversational second gear, astounded him with the announcement that he was desperately keen to get back to his desk, and dragged himself up the stairs again. A brief conversation, and not at all a satisfying one.

Working proved less easy than he'd anticipated. The excitement of the previous couple of days wrought havoc on his concentration. As did the pressure he was working under. As Flavia had pointed out to him, find that Raphael and all was well. The penalty for failure was not, however, merely a raised eyebrow from his supervisor this time. This is not, he told himself as he flipped through the books he'd ordered, what academic work is meant to be like. The marines would be less dangerous at the moment. It was all very well to say "find a Raphael." But if it was that easy, it would have been found years ago.

Of course, he'd made progress, but only of a negative sort. He knew better where the painting *wasn't.* That, however, was not going to bring him many congratulations. From the initial two hundred and something or other possibilities, it was now down to a few dozen. What was he meant to do? Visit every one with a sharp knife and give it a little scrape? Apart from the fact that the owners might protest, presumably someone else was also on the same course. If Byrnes had destroyed that picture so it wouldn't be revealed as a fake, he was smart enough to know he'd have to get rid of the real thing as well, which was the last possible proof of his initial fraud.

The idea made him think; he paid less attention to his books and stared up at the wire netting strung across the ceiling to stop falling bits of roof from the decaying building hitting the students below. The books didn't seem quite so important now. He could accumulate information for months, and still never find anything convincing. If he was going to get anywhere, he'd have to work with what information he already had. He had to find the picture to catch a culprit. But what if he did it the other way round? Lateral thinking, it was called, and once he started thinking along these lines, everything began to seem quite simple. And after a few hours, he even began to get a smell of where the picture might be.

LATER that evening he met Flavia on schedule and in the right place, and the two of them walked into a cutesy little wine-bar in a street running parallel to Wardour Street. It was called the Cockroach and Cucumber, or somesuch, which prompted Argyll to make a few disparaging comments. "It'll probably be full of the elder brothers of the students who work in the V & A," he sniffed at Flavia, who missed the reference and smiled politely. She'd had a tiresome day, talking to the other restorers. Not that it had done her much good. They'd all taken refuge in technicalities and refused to come out of their shells. This was her last chance to make the trip worthwhile. It made her determined, and sliced the edge off her sense of humour.

The clientele around the bar generated a rubicund air of confident and artificial jollity that settled around Argyll like a suffocating smog. He felt unhappy already. "Hardly the place for a quiet and confidential chat," he bellowed into Flavia's left ear.

"What?" she yelled back, then sighted the Tate restorer. "Doesn't matter. Tell me later." She weaved her way over to the bar. Anderson, her target, was standing there, waving a five-pound note in a hopeful fashion. Flavia rapped him on the shoulder firmly, just at the moment his long vigil was rewarded, and the barmaid was headed in his direction. He turned to greet the Italian, lost eye-contact with the other side of the bar, and the woman drifted off to serve someone else.

"Goddamn," he exclaimed. "Missed her again. No matter. We can go next door where it's quieter. They have table service through there."

As they walked through, Flavia introduced Argyll. Anderson looked disappointed. "Oh. I thought you were coming alone." Argyll was instantly offended and found himself disliking the man intensely. They sat down at one of the few remaining tables and ordered a bottle of white wine of uncertain origin. "You see? It's a lot quieter in here. Nice place, eh?"

Argyll smiled and nodded. "Remarkable. Nice is not the word." He'd wanted to say that for years. Flavia smiled at him and trod heavily on his toe with her heel. They were not called stilettos for nothing. Tears came into his eyes from the pain.

She then went on to try and rescue the conversation, parroting out a largely erroneous explanation of her presence in England.

"And you want my help. Willingly. If, of course, you tell me why."

"Just routine enquiries, as I believe they say in this country."

"Nonsense. Nothing I could possibly say would be of

the slightest use to you unless there was more to it than that. I knew nothing about the painting except that I was called in by Sir Edward Byrnes to clean and restore it. Apart from the occasional incursion by television cameras, I worked alone with the other restorers. Why send someone all the way from Rome just to ask about that?

"And of course, you turn up here bringing Mr. Argyll—" for some reason Argyll disliked that Mister bit, "—who Sir Edward once told me was miffed about the whole business. Why search for motives when you take the number one suspect along with you? Unless, of course, there is something else going on. Cheers." He raised his glass to salute his cleverness, and screwed his face up in an exaggerated demonstration of disgust.

"I never realised that I had achieved such fame," commented Argyll, uncertain whether Anderson's facial antics referred to the wine or him.

"Don't worry. You haven't. But Byrnes mentioned you once and I have a very good memory for minor details."

Argyll decided to retire from the conversation as much as possible. Minor details, indeed. He leant back in his chair, nursed his glass of wine, and tried to look nonchalant. If it hadn't been for his afternoon's labours he would be in a bad mood. However, what he had to tell Flavia made him feel smug. It would be agreeable to be in control of events for once.

"Will you give me your word that this conversation will be confidential?" Flavia asked.

"I can give you my word and you can decide how much

it's worth," Anderson replied. Flavia thought some more. She not only wanted information, it would be nice to rattle this little bugger's confidence a little. Suggesting he might have been one of the prime victims of a hoax might sober him up a bit. Also, she didn't like that crack about Argyll: maybe he had been a little objectionable, but basically she agreed with him. This worried her. Becoming protective was always a bad sign.

"It was a fake," she announced bluntly.

The statement did the trick nicely. Anderson didn't exactly turn pale, but clearly felt like it. "Oh shit," he said, very slowly and distinctly. "Are you sure?"

Flavia shrugged and smiled prettily at him, but didn't reply.

"And can you tell me why you think that?"

She shook her head. "No. I'm afraid not. Just take it that we're right." It was a gross and unreasonable exaggeration, but Bottando had always instructed her that the one golden rule about police work was never ever seem uncertain of your facts. Besides, she reckoned that the more upset Anderson was, the more he'd talk. She switched into concerned and attentive mode.

"I think I ought to buy you something to eat here. I'm pretty hungry."

So was Argyll. And he appreciated that the little gesture was, perhaps, a good way of establishing a better rapport with Anderson. He was the sort of tactless person who not only can't resist a free meal, but who is also made hungry by bad news. For the next hour he munched his way steadily through a large plate of jumbo prawns, a sizeable slice of fish pie, two plates of vegetables, a dessert that was meant to be pecan pie but wasn't quite right somehow, two cups of coffee and an unfair share of a second bottle of wine. Flavia also matched him pretty much forkful for forkful. As on the first occasion when he had watched her prowess in this field, Argyll wondered how on earth someone of such a delightfully trim shape could possibly stuff that much food inside her.

To help Anderson in the right direction, Flavia began telling him about the scientific study of the picture. The scientist waved her aside. "I know all this. I was in charge."

"I thought Manzoni was?"

"Him?" Anderson said contemptuously. "He never came near it. Just read the report afterwards, said he was sure we'd done it all correctly, and signed the thing. Scarcely lifted a finger."

Flavia was quite unjustifiably irritated at the aspersions cast on her fellow-countryman by this large and cocky Englishman. His comments smacked too much of anti-Italian prejudice for her taste. Moreover, it meant one of her pet theories was weakened. If Manzoni hadn't directed the tests, he couldn't have fixed them either. Her focus came back to Anderson, who was pronouncing at great length, not noticing she hadn't been paying any attention.

". . . That's why I'd like to hear your evidence. I can't see any way that picture could be a fake. It looked right and tested right. The evidence would have to be absolutely overwhelming to make me change my mind," he concluded.

She evaded again. "Just tell me, how would someone fake a thing like that?"

"In principle it's easy. It's just doing it that's the trouble. From what I remember of the report, the forger would have had to get hold of a sixteenth- or late fifteenth-century canvas to start off with. One the right size as the final picture so there wouldn't be any new strain marks from the new shape of the stretcher. You clean off some, but not all, of the original paint. Then you start painting your own picture, using the same techniques and the same paint recipes as the original artist."

Flavia nodded. So far what he was saying fitted in exactly with the jottings in the Swiss sketch-books.

"Once you've painted it, then it has to be artificially dried and aged. An oil painting takes years to dry completely, sometimes half a century. There's no bigger give-away than a Renaissance picture which is sticky. That, incidentally, is how Wacker, the Van Gogh forger, got caught in the 1930s.

"Drying can be done in several ways," he continued. "The traditional method is to bake it—preferred temperatures vary from forger to forger—then roll it up in several directions to crack the surface, then dip it in a solution of ink to darken the cracks and make them look dirty. That, at least, was the Van Meegeren method, and he was one of the greatest. Couldn't paint for tuppence, but a great forger.

"Of course, there are ways of checking all that. The Elisabetta was analysed for the way it had dried, the direction and type of the cracking were examined, bits of paint were scraped off and tested in a dozen different ways, the dirt boiled up and analysed chemically. All perfect, as I say."

"So you've told us how to get caught. How about not getting caught?" Argyll suggested.

"There are some ways, I suppose," Anderson replied reluctantly. "As far as drying goes, you might try a low-voltage microwave oven, perhaps. That would produce a different method of drying out. Not foolproof, by any means, but it wouldn't produce the tell-tale signs one looks for to indicate normal baking. Cracking is also relatively simple if you are careful to preserve the original pattern on the host painting. Doing it is incredibly hard, but it is possible.

"In the case of the Raphael, you could dissolve the dirt from the original painting in some solution of alcohol and spread that over the surface. When it was tested it would be seen as being of a mixture of different substances, which is what it should be. The alcohol would also show up, but in this case might be confused with the substances we used to clean the thing.

"But it's paint itself which proves it. It's difficult to see how to get round that, and we tested it endlessly. Spectroscope, electron microscope, dozens of different routines. There can be no doubt. It was sixteenth-century, Italian, painted with Raphael's techniques. Genuinely old paint. Not just new paint mixed with old recipes. Old paint. Everything worked out perfectly. Which is why I don't really believe it was a fake."

"I know how it was done," said Argyll quietly. They both looked at him. "It's just occurred to me. Flavia, you told me the tests on the paint were done from a thin, long strip from the left-hand side of the picture?" She nodded.

"So why couldn't the painter have left that bit from the original sixteenth-century picture? Paint over the central portion and match the background and portrait up. Then you could test to your heart's content, and the tests would have been positive every time."

"Is that possible?" Flavia asked Anderson.

He considered the matter. "Technically, I suppose so. Of course it would be a bit difficult to hide the joins from X-rays, but that might be done if you add a small amount of metallic salt to blur the picture. If I remember, there *was* some blurring, but we were in a hurry, it was a new machine, so everyone assumed it was just a glitch. The real problem with that interpretation is how could any forger be sure the right bit of paintwork was tested?"

"That was no trouble at all. You were *told* to test that bit, weren't you? And who told you, eh?"

"The museum did."

"You spoke to the museum yourself? They wrote to you?"

"No. Sir Edward told us. He said the museum didn't want any damage . . ."

"Aha." Argyll leaned back in his chair once more,

crossed his arms and nodded at Flavia. "There you are. Problem solved. Glad you brought me now?"

ARGYLL was in an excellent mood as he wandered round shops and libraries the next day, collecting the final bits and pieces he needed. In truth, the previous evening had been a triumph. Not only had he put that insufferable restorer in his place and come up with a nifty idea to prove Byrnes's guilt, he had compounded the achievement by giving Flavia his startling news as they walked back to the hotel she had chosen. He had, he told her, found the picture.

She was impressed. No doubt about it. Of course, she did insist on asking awkward questions like where was it? how had he tracked it down? and things like that. But he managed to sidestep those, saying mysteriously that she'd have to wait and see. That irritated her, but he stuck to his position. After all, he wasn't quite as sure as he'd implied.

So, whistling contently to himself, Argyll flitted in and out of art supply shops, accumulating equipment; and visited the literary-memoir, travel and history sections of the London Library, gathering an impressively filled plastic bag of possessions.

He looked at his watch. Eleven o'clock. Ten minutes to go, a brief visit to Byrnes as he'd arranged by telephone earlier that day, then back to Rome on the two o'clock flight. Perfect. He began to feel he was quite good at this sort of thing.

Inside the Byrnes Gallery he gave his name to the assistant, mentioned he had an appointment, and looked at the pictures while he waited. Five minutes later he was ushered into Byrnes's inner sanctum and shown to a seat. He declined the offer of a cup of coffee.

"Jonathan. I didn't know you were back in London quite so soon. How can I help you?" Byrnes smiled gently over the half-moon glasses he used for reading. Argyll disliked them; they always gave the wearer the opportunity to peer over them at you as if he was looking at some anatomical specimen. Very affected.

"Hardly at all," he said. "I was just passing so thought I'd drop in and say hello. Just to let you know I was around." He smiled inanely. He'd always been told he overdid the foolish look, but it came in decidedly useful now.

"And why are you around? I thought you would be hard at work in Rome by now. Or have you been roped into this Raphael business as well?"

Argyll shook his head with what he hoped was a look of despair. "Yes. Blasted thing. I curse the day I ever thought of it. The police of course suspect me, and you, and just about everyone else. So I'm here trying to work my way into their good books—by finding the real one." He said it lightly, then paused significantly, looking at the plaster ceiling as he did so.

Byrnes's left eyebrow shot up in a creditable look of

astonishment. He did it well. Argyll was all admiration. "The real one? What are you talking about?"

"Did the police not tell you?" Argyll said in surprise. "The picture was a fake. A genuine Jean-Luc Morneau, may he rest in peace. It'll be a very great scandal when it all comes out. If it does, that is." They looked at each other with the glimmerings of mutual understanding.

"If?"

"No proof, you see. Except for the picture, which isn't there any more. Manzoni might have known something . . ."

"But someone knifed him, it appears," Byrnes continued. He was now leaning on his desk, having abandoned the air of easy relaxation that had greeted Argyll on his entry. "I see."

"So now," Argyll continued, getting to the point in a circuitous fashion which, on the whole, seemed justified by results, "it's all up to me. I've been asked—told might be a better word—to find the original. Prove the first one was a fake. The police think this will lead to the culprit and to Manzoni's murderer. Simple."

"If you can do it," Byrnes pointed out.

"I already have," he said smugly.

"Where is it?"

Argyll paused once again. That, of course, was the crucial question. He was not meant to tell anyone at all about this. If Flavia ever discovered, ever even suspected, that he'd mentioned so much as a word of it to Byrnes, she'd clap him in jail without a second thought. Even alluding to the painting as a fake was bad enough. On the other hand, Argyll had to think about saving his own neck. Reaching a careful understanding with Byrnes about what was going to happen next seemed the best way of doing it. He took a deep breath and stepped off the edge.

"Siena," he said. "But I've been told not to go into details."

"Of course, of course," Byrnes replied reassuringly. "Quite proper." There was no need to go into details, of course. He could see that by the thoughtful look in Byrnes's eyes. He'd said enough. The rest was up to Byrnes.

The conversation dragged on for a few more minutes, then, pleading urgent business, Argyll got up, made his farewells and left.

12

BOTTANDO groaned with impatience as the telephone rang once again. He'd had a dreadful morning. His secretary, hand-picked for her ability to persuade callers to go away, was sick. The very defensiveness he complained about in Tommaso's secretary, he treasured in his own.

In her absence, all the calls came straight through to his phone. Bottando had never realised there were so many; he'd managed to achieve virtually nothing all day. At first, he'd attempted just to let the thing ring and pretend to be out, but he couldn't stand the thought of missing something important. Some of the calls, at least, had justified his weak will. He had been busy, although his colleagues would have been a little surprised at his occupation. He was reading through his old cases, a carefully stuck-down folder of newspaper clippings reporting on his past triumphs. The past failures, of course, he left out. Lots of policemen have such things; it works wonders for promotion to be able, casually of course, to hand over accounts of how wonderful, how zealous and how effective you've been. Even if the opinions are only those of journalists, it looks good.

So he had the folder, which he occasionally took down and flicked through for nostalgic reasons. It also boosted his confidence when things were not going so well. Look, the folder told him, don't worry, see what you've achieved before. He was reading through an account of his great triumph in the Milan financial scandal. It reassured him he hadn't lost his touch.

The phone rang once more, and once more he lifted the receiver. "*Pronto*Bottando," he said, all in one weary word.

"General, Ferraro here. I was wondering how the investigation was coming along."

Bottando repressed a sigh as best he could. The man had become as much a menace as Tommaso. If one was nervous and irritable, the other was showing signs of having a breakdown. It was about the tenth call in two days. No form of vagueness, obstruction or even downright rudeness seemed to put either of them off. They had become obsessed with the Raphael, its authenticity, and demands that the culprit be found. Both of them had a lot at stake. At least this time he had something to report.

"Quite well," he said. "My assistant has just rung to say that she is coming back to Rome this afternoon, bringing that man Argyll in tow. He seems to think he is making progress in the hunt for our missing artefact."

"Excellent. And where is it?"

"That I can't tell you, I'm afraid. Argyll is a man with an overdeveloped sense of drama. Flavia says he is keeping it as a surprise."

"Oh. Well, as long as he's right this time. His track record in these matters is not so good, after all." The voice on the other end of the line sounded disappointed.

"I appreciate your concern. We are also making some progress in other areas as well. But again, I can't tell you much, if you don't mind. Or rather, I'd prefer not to."

"That's quite all right. I understand. My concern is the Raphael. The criminal side of things is your business, I suppose. But please remember I want to be kept informed."

"How could I possibly forget? Don't worry. I'll come round to the museum later and brief you and the director fully."

It seemed worth trying as a way of deflecting further phone calls, anyway. Tiresome man. At least Tommaso was off the hook: he had an unbreakable alibi for Manzoni's murder. Dinner with the prime minister was fairly convincing. God only knew what they must have talked about. He shuddered at the thought. Ferraro had worked late in the museum and was seen leaving at nine o'clock, which seemed to take him out of the running, as well.

Bottando tried to get through some small routine tasks necessary to keep his superiors off his back, but abandoned the work after an hour. The phone was still going, and his head was starting to ring in sympathy. As was his stomach: he had not had any lunch yet, and it was already half three.

He went over to the bookshelf in his office, removed a thick volume, and walked out of the door. If he was going to read, he would do it in a restaurant, the book propped up on a roll of bread, with a plate of pasta in front of him. Where no more phone calls could disturb his peace for an hour.

THEY noticed him still sitting at his table in the Piazza del Collegio Romano, as they drove through in the taxi from the airport to the office. It was an eccentric route, but the driver insisted on the deviation, explaining that there was a demonstration at the end of the Corso and the more direct way was jammed solid with a screaming mass of protestors.

Flavia yelled to stop the taxi when she saw him, they paid, and joined him at his table. It was a restaurant he used often, one of the few that was willing to serve up food at such a late hour. In most, the diners had long since been hurried away, the tablecloths shaken off and the doors closed. For the tourists, who made up the majority of eaters at this time of year, there was little else to do for the next few hours but return to their hotels, sit on the edge of a fountain, or return to the foot-blistering work of hammering over the hard cobbles in search of more artistic delights.

Bottando fussed round them and insisted on summoning the waiter for some food. "You must be starving. Some good food will work wonders for you. I remember well what London restaurants are like." He made a good-natured face and beamed at Argyll, who was a little surprised at the amiable reception.

"Mr. Argyll, I'm pleased to meet you at long last. I gather you have made another great discovery. I hope you are right this time."

Argyll shrugged. "I think so. By a process of elimination I'm bound to get there eventually."

"It's the elimination bit that worries me. Must it be taken so literally?"

Argyll laughed a little awkwardly, and Bottando politely suspended the conversation while they ate. "What's that you've got there?" Flavia enquired.

"This? Oh, this is the bible." He read them the spine of his book, "*Who's Who in Art.* A positive treasure trove of useful information. Full of unsuspected details about our friends, colleagues and enemies."

He flicked through some pages. "Take, for example, my dear friend Spello. To look at him you'd never suspect he was once a senior advisor to the Vatican, back in the 1940s, would you? Such an unkempt man. And they're such snappy dressers at the Vatican. He must have been very young. I imagine he considered he had a great career ahead of him, rather than merely a secondary position buried in Etruscan statuary. Or that our beloved minister, a very lumpy dolt of military aspect and no apparent delicacy whatever, has a passion for bonsai gardening? Or that Tommaso's secret desire is to be a painter?"

"It says that?"

"Not exactly. But he told me he plans to retire and paint at his villa, and it says here that he once trained at an art school. In Lyons, no less. So, I conclude that he really wanted to be a painter. Evidence plus logical analysis. That's detection."

"And now I suppose you are going to say he was wonderful at it and made a particular study of Raphael?"

"No, Flavia, no. Would that it were so simple and easy. Alas, poor man, I think he was probably not good at all, and had the sense to look after the paintings of others rather than create his own. Besides, one of the few things we've established is that, if it was a fake, then Morneau was the faker. What we need now is proof of something. Which is a task you seem to have taken upon yourselves. So, tell me. Where is it?"

"Siena," Argyll replied simply. Bottando looked surprised. "Are you sure? How do you come to that conclusion?"

"Because it's the only conclusion to come to. It wasn't in the Clomorton collection, it wasn't in the di Parma collection, and it has disappeared. Therefore . . ."

"Therefore . . . ?" prompted Bottando.

Argyll looked superior. "I don't think I'll tell you. I

might still be wrong. Anyway, you have the facts. You can work the rest out yourself. Evidence plus logical analysis, General. That's detection."

"Very funny. Still, as long as I know where you're going, and as long as you find the thing, I suppose the details can wait. Are you going up there?"

"Tomorrow morning. I don't think there's any need to rush up immediately. I think it's quite safe for the time being," Flavia answered, then broke off to order a coffee. It would play havoc with her stomach juices, but she reckoned she needed something to sip.

"*It* may be, but you may not. Some protection might be a good idea when you go," Bottando continued.

Flavia shook her head again. "No. If we go roaring up the autostrada in a fleet of armed police cars there'll be an enormous fuss. Initially it'll be much better to go up quietly and check the thing out. Then you can put as many armed guards around us as you like. The more the better, in fact. But if we go clomping about the place like that, someone will talk. And it'll be all over the newspapers tomorrow morning. Just make sure you keep it to yourself."

"Yes. You are possibly right. What time will you go?"

"First thing tomorrow morning. Before that I need to draw some money, make out an expenses slip to catch the deadline for the next paycheck, have a nice shower, and collect some clothes."

"Tell me where to find you. Oh, by the way, you might

want to look at this." He reached into his jacket and pulled out a sheet of paper.

"Telex from Janet. Poor man complains about having to do so much work for us, but don't let that concern you. I'm sure he got someone else to do it for him. He's been tracking down picture-buying. Score, Byrnes three, Morneau six, everybody else, nil."

"May I?" said Argyll, reaching over to take it. He unfolded it and read the communication carefully.

"That's it. That must be it." He pointed at a line of type after a few moments' perusal. " 'Portrait of a lady, copy after Fra Bartolommeo.' Three thousand Belgian francs, to Jean-Luc Morneau. Seventy centimetres by a hundred and forty. Right size, more or less, and about the right age. Right style. That would have been perfect. Your colleague didn't send a photograph as well, did he?" he asked hopefully.

Bottando rummaged around in his pockets once more. "Yes," he said, handing over another sheet of paper. "Not very good, I'm afraid. Just a photocopy from the sale catalogue. Pretty good service though, don't you think?"

Argyll was too busy looking at it to reply. He handed it over to Flavia, a satisfied look on his face. She looked disappointed. It was, in truth, unimpressive: very dirty, a three-quarter-length of a large middle-aged woman with a prospective double chin and a few other obvious attractions. Dressed in a dark, full-sleeved dress. Black hair, as far as he could tell through the dirt, and overloaded with vulgar jewellery: a tiara, a vast necklace and a thick, intricate ring.

"Not a great loss if it was used. The portrait of Elisabetta he put on top was much better," she commented.

"True. But look at the window and external scenery in the left background. Very similar to the fake Raphael, and exactly where the tests were taken. I think that's pretty conclusive, myself."

Bottando nodded approvingly. "You've got a good eye," he said. "I noticed the same thing myself, with a photograph of the Raphael to help."

"Which proves Morneau painted it, and that lets Spello off the hook," Flavia added with satisfaction.

"Alas, no. Morneau was also an advisor to the Vatican, back in the 1940s, and he must have known Spello then. That's one example of why these books are so useful."

He got up and brushed breadcrumbs from his lap. "Time to get back to the office. I have to work even if you two don't."

They parted, Flavia and Argyll heading east, while Bottando walked back to the office. He was worried. He hadn't mentioned it to Flavia, not only because Argyll was there, but also because he didn't want to concern her unnecessarily. But he knew he was about to take a huge risk with them. And it concerned him greatly.

LESS burdened with cares than Bottando, Flavia and Argyll spent a delightful evening, once the business of washing themselves and their clothes, and other domestic matters had been taken care of. Flavia had put on the washing machine, opened her mail and fussed about the apartment while Argyll had read some of the books he had brought with him.

While he sat with his leg over the arm of her one comfortable seat, he read out extracts from the books he was looking through. This was a change from the plane flight home, when he had read intensely and said scarcely a word. Flavia had noticed that a guide book to the Palazzo Pubblico in Siena had been one of the volumes.

Argyll laughed. "Listen to this. It's a letter from Viscount Perceval about Lady Arabella. A great diarist and observer of eighteenth-century London, that man. She gets more and more remarkable every time I come across her. It wasn't only husband two who had wayward habits. Number one also couldn't keep his hands to himself either. She broke a cello over his head at a royal levee because of it. Then tried to beat him up with her fists. In public. Must have made everybody's evening."

Or later: "Another bit. Clomorton told the Duchess of Albemarle he was in love with a 'dark-haired beauty.' That was a mistake, poor sod. He must have known she was the worst tattletale in London. Perceval says she wrote to Lady Arabella directly. That must be what she was talking about in that letter I read you in London. Think of the reception the poor man would have got. Luckily for him he dropped dead first."

"What are you reading this for? Does it have anything to do with Siena?"

"No. I was just looking to see if there was any mention of Sam Paris, Raphael or whatever. A very arty man, Perceval, and a great observer of the London scene. Nothing happened without him noticing it and jotting it down in his diary. A Raphael on the market, or a scandal about one, would be in here somewhere. There isn't, which makes me more convinced I'm right."

"Are you going to tell me? Or am I to be treated like the General?"

He took her hand and kissed it absentmindedly, letting go when he realised what he'd done. "Silly. Of course not. After dinner you will hear all."

They had ended up digesting their evening meal by walking blissfully around the city. Flavia pointed out to Argyll her favourite buildings and spots; they had wandered around the old ghetto, looking affectionately at the run-down buildings, Imperial fragments and tranquil, beautiful piazzas that suddenly appear as you turn unpromising-looking corners. Argyll gave an impromptu disquisition on the beauties of the Farnese Palace. Flavia wasn't entirely persuaded, but liked his sense of conviction. She had responded by dredging through the memories of her university days and identifying all the large medallions on the Palazzo Spada a little down the road.

"I can do that too," Argyll said. "Come with me." He grabbed her hand and led her to the other side of the Piazza Farnese, down the via Giulia and then left down a side street. He pointed to an emblem above one of the large wooden gates that shut prying eyes from the courtyard beyond. "There. Two pelicans intertwined, surmounted by a crown and the symbol of a castle. Whose is it?"

Flavia chewed her lip for a moment. "Don't know. Whose?"

"That's the di Parma symbol. This was their Roman palace."

She grinned. "So this is where it all started. I knew the palace was around here somewhere, but I never got around to looking. What's in there now?"

"Just apartments, I imagine. It looks very tatty. The point is, however, that Mantini lived there, which explains why he was brought in for this job in the first place." Argyll pointed to a door a few yards up on the other side of the street.

"As for the picture," he went on, "the di Parmas didn't have it, nor the Clomortons, nor the dealer Sam Paris. Mantini was the only man involved who was left. Lots of motive as he was always hard up. Or maybe love of the painting was more important and he didn't want it to leave Italy and be bought by a clod like Clomorton. So he paints over the Raphael, makes a copy of the same picture which he gives to the dealer, and keeps the real thing himself.

"He couldn't uncover it either, because he lived almost next door to the di Parmas, who might have got upset. But there'd be no rush if he wanted the picture for itself, not the money it could bring. So it could sit there and wait until he retired back to his home town, or something.

"But he never made it to retirement. He has a seizure and dies in 1727, at the age of fifty-two. Perfect health, just drops dead one afternoon in the street. No time, you see, for deathbed confessions or secret instructions about his picture. His daughter inherits his small fortune and remaining pictures. She returns to her father's native *paese*, where she marries a silversmith."

"Siena."

"Quite right. And he, because silversmiths were highly thought of, gets on the town council and dies, wealthy and greatly respected, in 1782. And he leaves to the city a couple of pictures. One portrait of himself, naturally, and the other a memento of that great Sienese painter, his own father-in-law, the superlative Carlo Mantini."

"Very good. But how do you know it's the right one?"

"Because it must be. Process of elimination. It's a ruin, which fits in with the evidence available, and it's the only picture which could possibly have concealed the Raphael."

This was the weak spot in an otherwise convincing argument, the area his supervisor would have pounced on, had he been there to listen. But he wasn't, and Flavia said nothing, so he hurried on. "I did about a month's work in a day and a half. Quite a lot of shortcuts, I admit. But if no one else has it, and they appear not to, it's the only other possibility. I hope you're proud of me."

Flavia patted him on the back. "Well done. Now all we have to do is go there and see if you're right. Come on. Let's go home."

13

FLAVIA and Argyll set out for Siena at eight sharp the next morning, Argyll in the passenger seat, Flavia driving her old but well-maintained Alfa Spider like a banshee. In a brief moment of feminine submissiveness she had suggested that Argyll might drive. In a long-standing tradition of English cowardice, he had declined. Nothing, he declared as they forced their way onto the main northern artery, would ever get him to drive in Rome. Not after the last time.

It was a wise decision. Flavia drove with knowledge, skill and determination; Argyll would have driven with his eyes shut. The maniacal early morning traffic died away to something more human fairly quickly, and they made rapid progress north.

It's a long, five-hour voyage to Siena, even if you drive—as Flavia did—far too fast on the motorway. It's also a very beautiful trip. The autostrada, one of the best in the country and one of the longest in Europe, starts outside Reggio di Calabria at the very tip of the south-western peninsula. It curls through the parched hills of the south to Naples, then turns up through the poor country-side of Calabria and Latium to Rome. Then it heads for Florence and swings east, through a series of giant tunnels and dizzying climbs, over the Apennines to Bologna. Here it splits, one arm reaching out to Venice, the other travelling on to Milan.

Even on the relatively small segment between Rome and Siena, it takes the traveller within easy reach of some of the most wonderful places in the world: Orvieto, Monte-fiascone, Pienza and Montepulciano; the Umbrian hill-towns of Assisi, Perugia, Todi, Gubbio. The stepped hills of vines and lowland pastures of goats and sheep mix perfectly with the rivers, the steep drops, and the dozens of often largely ignored medieval fortress-towns, perched on top of their protective hills as if the Medicis still reigned supreme.

It was wonderful. Argyll had travelled around Italy for years, had seen nearly all the major sights several times over, but never tired of seeing them all again. For a brief interlude, he forgot his woes, enjoyed the scenery and tried to pay no attention to his companion's driving.

Five hours almost to the minute later, they swung off the motorway, paid the fee at the toll and headed down the hilly road through Rapolano to Siena, having spent their journey in a mood of cheerful contentment and buoyant optimism. Contentment on Argyll's part, optimism on Flavia's. Then Argyll said: "How are we going to go about this little expedition? After all, we can hardly wander into the palazzo, take the picture off the wall and attack it with a knife. Curators don't like that. It upsets them."

"Don't worry. I thought about it last night. We'll just go and make sure it's still there, then make an official visit tomorrow."

They were a little delayed getting to their hotel. Siena is a town where the streets have changed not at all since the thirteenth century, and to cope with modern traffic flows, the authorities have instituted one of the most ferociously complex one-way systems ever devised. A single mistake anywhere, and you are flung off in entirely the wrong direction without the slightest chance of doing anything about it. They had driven—quite illegally as the area is closed to traffic—past the cathedral twice before Flavia reversed the wrong way down a narrow one-way street and found the road she wanted at the end.

She had chosen a comfortable, elegant and expensive hotel to serve as their temporary headquarters. It also served a remarkable lunch, which Argyll suspected might have weighed more heavily in its favour. They had a preliminary drink, and Argyll leaned back in his chair to gaze at the Tuscan hills out of the window. "Wonderful," he said. "The Italian police really do things in style."

Flavia shrugged. "The very last thing the General said to me was that we were to take care of ourselves."

"I don't think this is quite what he had in mind."

She spread her hands out wide in a very Italian gesture. "Who can tell? Find this picture and no one will care. Besides, I've always wanted to stay in this place. And my expenses in London were derisory. This will make up for it a little. I've booked us in over the weekend. We can sort the picture out, then have a couple of days relaxing. Do you mind?"

"Am I complaining? This time last month I was sitting in a sandwich shop in London eating a cheese and pickle roll. This arrangement seems slightly preferable, whatever the dire consequences of failure."

"Are you afraid of that?"

"Of failing or the consequences? Yes and no. I think you will have your proof by tomorrow, whatever happens. Do you carry a gun, by the way?"

Flavia frowned at the apparent *non sequitur*, trying to work out the mental leaps that took her companion from one subject to another. "No," she said, giving up the effort. "I'm not in the police, remember. Just a civilian. Why do you ask?"

He shook his head and smiled at her reassuringly. "No reason. Just wondering. This painting has been unlucky."

Getting back to a more comfortable topic, Flavia announced that they had more than enough time for lunch, and that, speaking personally, she needed some. Then they examined the local church, slowly and in a relaxing fashion, and walked, equally gently, into the centre. Striding up the hill was a little tiring, Argyll not having had much in the way of exercise for months, and his enjoyment of the stroll was spoiled by his trying to seem not too much out of breath. Flavia seemed not at all affected by the incline.

They reached the Campo at four, after a brief pause while Flavia did some shopping. How she could think of shopping at a time like this was beyond him, but he put it all down to cultural relativism. Some people do odd things to work off tension, and despite their relaxing start, he could tell that both of them were starting to feel just a little nervous.

The square they were heading for is a bizarre shape, like the outline of a cup, which runs downhill from the curved portion to a flat plane at the end. The straight side is almost entirely taken up by the palace; the centre of administration back in the days when Siena was a major city-state whose power, briefly, rivalled that of Florence itself.

The days of greatness had long since gone, however. A couple of unfortunate sixteenth-century decisions concerning the choice of enemies, a rapid war, and Siena settled into the role of minor provincial backwater. Since the seventeenth century, when some wise burgher had the bright idea of inventing the Palio—the annual horse race round the Campo—it had survived mainly on tourist income.

This year's contingent was beginning to flow in nicely. All the numerous cafés along the curved sides at the top of the Campo had laid out their chairs, tables and umbrellas, and waiters were flitting to and fro, delivering glasses of pastis, coffees, bottles of mineral water and the inevitable Coca-Colas. Little posses of tourists stood around gaping at the sight, or heading for the entrance to the palace.

There was not a lot of time to admire the view. Flavia led Argyll rapidly to the palazzo entrance, paid the two thousand five hundred lire entrance fee and wasted a few minutes complaining to the ticket seller about the disgraceful expense. This preliminary over, they crossed the courtyard and set about being sightseers. They had timed it quite well. Most Italian museums stop admitting new visitors at about twenty-five minutes before closing time; they had bought their tickets with five minutes to spare.

In the lower hall, where the great frescos by Sodoma are displayed, they split up, Flavia to examine the doors and windows, Argyll to locate the Mantini. An unpleasant shock awaited him when he arrived in the upper saloon. According to the picture in his guide book, 1975 edition, the picture should have been in a dark corner at the back, above a glass case of miscellaneous Renaissance silverware and just to the left of a vast nineteenth-century painting of Vittorio Emanuele, unifier of Italy, striking a heroic pose on a horse.

It wasn't. Instead, there was a group of early twentieth-century town councillors, done in the degenerate style of portraiture that proved that Italy was long since past its best in the picture department. Argyll's heart sank. After his enormous confidence that his plan would go off smoothly, he was now going to have to explain himself. This would be a little hard for Flavia to swallow. He could almost see the stern look of disapproval on her face, and her opinion of him dwindling into nothing as he told her.

He walked over to the guardian of the room, took out his guide book and jabbed his finger at the photograph. "You see this picture? Where is it? I've come all the way from England just to see it, and it's not there."

The guardian looked at him pityingly. "You came from England to see *that*? Listen: take my advice. Go downstairs to the *Mappamondo*. It's much better, one of the finest things in all Siena."

"I know that," Argyll retorted testily, feeling his aesthetic integrity was being impugned, "But I want to see this. Where has it gone to?"

The guard shrugged. "How should I know? I've only been working here a few weeks. I only know what's in here. Go next door and ask Enrico."

He did as he was told and found Enrico, a man of at least sixty, sitting lifelessly on a wooden chair by the door, staring without any sort of interest at the tourists coming and going. He did not look like a man who enjoyed his work overmuch. Argyll explained that Giulio had sent him, and did he know where this was?

Enrico looked at the picture. "Oh. That. Yes, that went years ago. The curator reckoned it was cluttering up the room. They took it down when the room was restored. He didn't want anything before 1850 in there."

Argyll was annoyed. "They took this down and left that monstrosity of Vittorio Emanuele up? That's a disgrace."

"That's different. It's after 1850. Besides, it's so big it won't go anywhere else." The guard shrugged again. The little fads of curators was evidently not a subject that enlivened him.

"Where's it now, then?"

The guard looked at the picture again and frowned. "Tower room," he said. "Don't know why everyone's so interested in that, all of a sudden. No one's shown the slightest concern about it for years. Listen, why don't you go downstairs and look at the *Mappamondo*. It's one of the finest . . ."

"Everyone? What do you mean? Someone else asked about it? When?" Argyll interrupted the sales pitch in panic.

"About an hour ago. Man came in here and asked the same question as you did. Sent him up to the tower room, too."

"Who was he?"

"You think I'm on first name terms with every visitor who comes here? How should I know?" The guard turned to bellow at some Germans on the other side of the room, and moved away. They weren't doing anything wrong, but Italian museum guards don't seem to like Germans overmuch. Besides, it ended a conversation he clearly found tedious.

Jesus, why the hell didn't he tell me that in the first place, Argyll thought as he ran desperately up the two flights of twisting stone stairs to the tower room. It was a long way up, and the last room *en route* to the great Campanile that dominates both the Campo and all of Siena. He arrived breathless, in a small bare room, crowded with faded and dirty prints and a jumble of pictures. There was a small table of inlaid wood in the centre. It was evidently where the museum stored the pictures it thought no one wanted to see. Most people probably walked straight through on their way to the platform at the top, three hundred feet above the square below.

His anxieties faded a little. It was still there, at least. He had not been outmaneuvered yet. There, in one corner, surrounded by old maps of Siena in glass frames, was an undoubted, genuine piece of the *oeuvre* of Carlo Mantini. It was a landscape, which was a little awkward. Typical stuff: a stream in the middle background, and a few blobs of paint signifying peasants tending sheep or goats. Speaking personally, he wouldn't have called it a landscape with ruins. But, a small hill on the right had a ruined castle on it, which revived his flagging confidence a little. The sky was clear and, had it not been so dirty, would have been a light blue. All of Mantini's skies were light blue. He couldn't paint them any other way.

Argyll stared at it with adoration. There it was. What a beautiful piece. What a gem. What a masterwork. He squinted at it. Looked a little smaller than it should, but that might be the effect of the frame. A pity it would have to be a touch damaged, but he was sure Mantini wouldn't mind if he knew what it would do for his only biographer's career. And it was going to be famous, if all went well.

He was still staring when a deafening alarm went off. "Christ, please, not a fire," was his initial reaction. Then it occurred to him it must be the bell to warn visitors that the museum was closing. He ran down the stairs again, a much easier task, and went searching for Flavia. She was standing in the main council room.

"Where have you been? I've been standing here for hours."

"Nonsense. We only arrived twenty minutes ago. I was looking for the picture. They moved it upstairs. Listen, he's here. He followed us. The guard told me someone was asking about the picture. What do we do now?"

She looked very alarmed at his urgent tone. "Who's here?"

"Byrnes."

"The picture's not been touched?" He shook his head. "Good." She walked around in little circles and rubbed her chin thoughtfully. "We've no choice," she said decisively after a few moments. "We'll have to go ahead now. It's too risky to go outside and wait until tomorrow. Come on."

She headed off. "Where are you going?" he called after her.

"Just to the toilet. Don't worry."

ARGYLL'S leg was long since dead of any sensation. He moved awkwardly, trying to get comfortable.

"Was this the best you could think of?" he asked peevishly.

Flavia was sitting on his knee. "Keep quiet. I think it's perfect. They've inspected the place already. They won't come again. Now we just have to sit tight for another three hours or so."

"Three hours? We've been here for days already. It's all right for you. You've got my warm comfortable knee to sit on. I'm the one wedged into this damned lavatory seat. And you might have said, then I could've eaten more lunch. I'm starving."

"Stop complaining. You were all secretive so why couldn't I be? Besides, I told you to eat up. Here, I bought this in the shop."

She reached down by the side of the toilet bowl, picked up her handbag and fished out a bar of chocolate.

"Why are you so certain the alarms won't go off? We're going to be very unpopular if we're arrested. Wouldn't it have been easier to flash your ID card and ask to examine it?"

"And have everybody know within hours? You know as well as I do that people in the art world are incapable of keeping their mouths shut. Besides, if we wait, it might not be here tomorrow. Anyway, we won't be caught. The guards will only be round once more; I checked the rota in the entrance. And the alarms are only on the entrances and exits. Obviously they think that any robber will try and get away. We won't. We just examine the picture, wait until morning, go out with the first visitors, phone

Bottando, and finish. There won't be anything missing, so no one will notice."

"We've got to spend all night here?" he hissed in horror. "In a women's toilet? Why not the men's, at least?"

"Yuck. What a dreadful idea. Dirty beasts, men."

Argyll ate his chocolate morosely. "Couldn't we just forget the Mantini?" he asked hopefully, trying to get his plan back on course. "After all, with Byrnes here, that's enough. I think we should just nip off to the hotel, call Bottando, have Byrnes arrested and come back in the morning." He finished the chocolate and remembered he'd omitted to offer her any.

"What makes you think it's Byrnes? The guard didn't describe him or anything like that."

"Well," said Argyll dubiously. "It must be, mustn't it? I mean, it stands to reason . . ."

"Not at all. All we know is that someone asked about that picture. Byrnes is the last person it could be. There's no way he could have found out where we are."

Argyll shifted uncomfortably on the toilet seat as she spoke. She took a hard look at him, an uneasy feeling coming over her.

"Jonathan? What have you done, damn you?"

"It's just that I thought, that, well . . . I told him, that's all."

Flavia didn't reply, but leant her forehead against the cool white tiles of the cubicle. "What did you do that for?" she asked faintly when she'd recovered herself.

"It seemed a good idea," he explained feebly. "You see,

even if we found the picture, it wouldn't get us any further in finding who was responsible. So I thought, if I told Byrnes, he'd have to do something about it. He'd come trotting out to Siena, and the police could arrest him as he entered the city."

"And you didn't think it worth mentioning this before? Perhaps it just slipped your memory? One of those little details, of no significance, that you just forgot about? You great dolt."

"Of course I didn't forget," he protested, his voice rising in pitch as he realised that his masterstroke wasn't getting the appreciation it deserved.

"Don't squeak at me like that."

"Well, why not? I'm getting tired of this," he continued—might as well let off steam now—"Everything I've done so far you've taken as evidence of my guilt. You're rude, objectionable and too clever for your own good. Obviously I couldn't tell you what I planned. You would have locked me up. And if we're now in a mess, it's just as much your fault as mine. If you hadn't known best all the time, and maybe trusted me a little more, I would have been more forthcoming. Besides which . . ."

"Oh, no. Don't say that. I hate it when you say that. Besides what?"

Argyll positively squirmed, as much as any man can when sandwiched between a lavatory seat and a semi-official member of the Italian police. He shouldn't have said it. His burst of wounded indignation had been very impressively delivered, and now he'd gone and spoiled the effect.

"Besides which," he went on reluctantly, "I'm not entirely convinced I've got the right picture. I think I have," he hurried on before she could say anything, "but I did say I had to cut a few corners."

"God preserve me," Flavia said quietly, to no one in particular. "We're up here, possibly on a fool's errand. Bottando is fast asleep in Rome and knows nothing about it. You appear to have successfully lured a murderer here without bothering to get any protection at all either for us or the picture. Well done. A fine achievement."

"I'll protect you," Argyll said gallantly, hoping to make some form of amends.

"Gee. Thanks, mister. That makes me feel a lot better." She would have continued in this vein, but felt it hardly worth wasting her breath.

ARGYLL had lapsed into a sullen, morose silence and ate his way steadily through the contents of Flavia's handbag. She had stocked it with enough food to withstand a siege. He desperately craved a cigarette.

Flavia had also lost her conversational flair. Clearly little could be done to repair their once promising relationship until that picture had been looked at. Then, perhaps, all would be forgotten and forgiven. He still thought it was a good plan, and was a little hurt that she'd reacted so badly. Maybe she was jealous of him for thinking it up?

When she finally decided that it was safe and time to go, it took about ten minutes to restore life to his leg. When he stood up for the first time, it collapsed under him and he fell, knocking over a large bucket with a toilet brush in it. It rattled over the floor, and the noise echoed around the room. They watched as it rolled slowly to a halt in the corner. "Be quiet, for God's sake," Flavia yelled in fright.

"You're making as much noise as I am. At least I'm not shouting my head off," he hissed back.

"I don't want us to get caught now. It would be very embarrassing."

He smiled in a half-way attempt to be conciliatory. "I'm sorry. I'm not used to this sort of escapade. It's not included in the introductory course for art history graduates."

She glared at him, still not ready to forgive. "Just keep quiet, all right? Now, let's get going."

She poked her head into the corridor, then disappeared through the door, gesturing for him to follow. They walked down to the main saloon again, and tiptoed, quietly and cautiously, over to the door that led to the staircase. It opened. No alarms. That at least was one worrying part over.

Once on the top floor, she flicked on a small torch, another purchase from the shop. "Now tell me I don't think of everything," she murmured to him as they walked. She went lightly and without a sound. Argyll, wearing his usual heavy, metal-tipped brogues, clattered after, despite all attempts to keep quiet. Had she mentioned she was proposing amateur cat burglary, he would have dressed appropriately.

The room was as he had left it six hours earlier. Flavia went over, quietly closed the heavy wooden shutters over the windows, and flipped the metal fastener to keep them secure. Then she closed the door, and pushed down the light switch.

"There. I don't see why we shouldn't be able to see what we're doing for a bit. No one will be along here for at least an hour. How long will this take you?"

"Not long at all," he replied as they gently took the picture off the hook that kept it on the wall and blew off the thin coat of dust all over it. "I'll have to be careful, but no more than five minutes, I reckon."

He had taken a book on the restoration and cleaning of pictures out of the library and had read the subject up on the plane flight. In principle it was simple. You just needed some form of solvent and a cloth. Then you brushed away until the right amount of dirt or paint was removed.

He pulled the tools he had bought in the art supply shop in London out of his pocket. A very small but very sharp knife, a large bundle of cotton wool and a small aerosol. "Combination of acid and alcohol. The man in the shop said it's the best thing you can buy." He grinned at her. "I think of everything, you see." No response.

As is often the case, practice turned out to be more complex than principle suggested. Argyll wanted to be careful not to do too much damage to the painting; after all, he was no restorer and had only the vaguest idea of what he was doing. So he concentrated on a very small amount of canvas in the bottom-left corner. But this meant he could only spray a small squirt from the aerosol at any time, in case it spread out too far.

So he settled down to squirt and rub, squirt and rub, only removing a tiny amount of dirt, varnish and paint at a time. It was hard work that required a lot of concentration. Every time he swabbed the cotton wool over the canvas, he hoped to see the tell-tale signs that indicated a masterpiece underneath.

"How's it going? You've been at it for nearly twenty minutes now." She spoke quietly but urgently, leaning against a table a few feet away to give him light. She rubbed her arms. "It's freezing in here."

He rubbed for another five minutes, the pile of dirty cotton-wool balls getting ever bigger. Then, as he gently slid a new ball across the paintwork, he stopped, and stared intently, scarcely believing his eyes.

"What is it? Have you found it?" She spoke excitedly, leaning forward for a better view.

"Paint," he said. "Green paint underneath . . . Flavia, put that light back on. What are you doing?"

Flavia didn't hear the rest of the sentence. The room was plunged into darkness. If both of them hadn't been concentrating so hard on the picture, they might have noticed the movement of the door opening. But they didn't, and the first time Flavia realised something was wrong was when she was hit on the side of the head with a thick length of wood. She fell on the floor, silent, with blood flowing swiftly from a broad cut in her scalp.

Argyll looked up at the sound, saw her collapse, and saw a shadowy figure advancing towards him. "Oh my God . . ." he began, but had no time to finish the remark. He had never been kicked in the stomach before, certainly not that hard, and had never imagined that anything could hurt so much.

Badly winded, he doubled up in agony, clutching at his stomach as though that might lessen the torment. He was pushed away from the picture and fell heavily on the floor. He liked, later, to think that he was moaning softly. In truth, his groans were probably a good deal louder. He didn't notice; his stomach fully occupied his consciousness, but he did reach out and touch Flavia, afraid of what he might discover.

"Don't you dare die on me. Keep going or I'll kill you," he whispered in her ear. He felt for her pulse, and couldn't find it. But he'd never been able to find his own either. He reached for her head and brushed her hair lightly, and felt the soft breath coming from her mouth and nose. She was still alive. But she wouldn't be for long unless he got his act together here. Nor would he, for that matter. "Looks like neither of us thought of everything," he said to her sadly.

Try as he might, he couldn't move. The pain was too

intense. All he could do was watch as the dark outline of the man who had given him such misery took a small, and evidently very sharp, knife and cut the painting, swiftly and without fuss, out of the back of the frame. At least, he assumed that was what was going on; all he could see was the occasional glint of metal. He didn't like the look of that knife, which was evidently a versatile instrument which could be put to many uses. He wheezed on the floor as the man rolled up the canvas, put it in a cardboard tube, and sealed it. Very methodical, in no rush at all.

That done, he picked up his knife again. "Oh, Lord," thought Argyll. "Here we go." He exploded from his sitting position and cannoned into the man's chest, knocking him off balance by sheer fluke. It used up all the reserves of energy and will-power he had. More, in fact. Men with knives can bring out the best in you.

But it was immediately obvious that his best wasn't enough. His antagonist slipped over, but Argyll simply didn't have the resources to do what was plainly required; that is, leap decisively up and down on his head with his heavy, metal-tipped shoes. Instead, he just stood there, still half hunched over with pain as his opponent rolled over, recovered his knife and began coming towards him again.

There was only one course left, and he took it. In the gloom, he could dimly make out that the infernal creature was between him and the door leading to the staircase down. So Argyll dashed through the other one and began to climb up. It was the best he could do to fulfil his promise to Flavia to protect her, even though she'd plainly been dismissive of his offer. With luck her assailant would follow him, giving Flavia a chance to regain consciousness and raise the alarm.

I *hope* he comes after me, anyway, he thought as he wheezed and puffed his way up the stairs. But what if he does something to Flavia first? Maybe I should have stayed down there.

It was a noble thought, and the fact that it was plainly impractical didn't make him feel less awful. He would have been killed and Flavia would have followed soon after. Which may yet be the case anyway, Argyll reflected.

He ran blindly up the stairs in the pitch dark, half-tripping, missing steps, but going as fast as he could. It got harder and harder. Earlier in the afternoon even the climb up the hill had been enough to wind him; the way he felt now, the man behind wasn't even going to have to bother sticking in a knife. It was what came of sitting in libraries when he should have been out jogging away and lifting weights. If he survived this, Argyll promised himself, he'd buy a rowing machine. The next time some tall, dark forger tried to knife him in a Sienese tower in the middle of the night, he'd be prepared for it. Up the stairs like the wind, he'd go.

His thoughts were getting confused from the combination of fright, pain and cramps. At one stage he stopped climbing. Doing so scared him to death, but he simply couldn't go on. He listened over the whistling, rasping sound of his breath; the soft pad of footsteps was just audible. He evidently had a lead, and his pursuer didn't seem to be hurrying. But then, why should he?—Argyll thought with a flash of despair—it's not as if I can get away. Perhaps he's as out of condition as I am?

The thought of his pursuer keeling over with a heart attack halfway up the stairs cheered him momentarily, but dissipated as he realised it was hardly likely. Whoever it was, the man with the hefty kick was not Sir Edward Byrnes—an elderly gent who, whatever the circumstances, would hardly go around kicking people in the stomach. He could just about see Byrnes knifing someone, but this sort of crawling around with wooden clubs and boots and knives didn't really seem the man's style.

Argyll began climbing the stairs again. He was going slowly, but making progress. The apparent inevitability of death doesn't mean that you will do nothing to postpone it for as long as possible. He doggedly kept on going to the top. Had circumstances been different, he could have stared at the view from the parapet for a very long time: bent double over the wall, choking as he dragged air into his much abused and protesting lungs, he saw the whole of Siena laid out like something out of a fairytale. A crescent moon illuminated the Campo and the jumble of medieval buildings around it. It lit up the black and white marble stripes of the cathedral tower. Twinkling lights from dozens of windows showed where the town's inhabitants were still up and about, watching the television, drinking wine, talking with friends. A light, warm and refreshing breeze. Beautiful, safe and normal.

But Argyll was in no mood to ponder over either the

scenery or his unfortunate situation. I could shout, scream bloody murder from the rooftops, he thought. But he didn't. No one would work out where it was coming from in time. And anyway, in the state he was in at the moment, he doubted that he could raise much more than a faint squeak.

He turned round at the creak of the door. The man was standing, quietly and still in the doorway, evidently evaluating how best to go about things. When Argyll had seen Flavia collapsing in a bloody heap, he had initially been furious, then desperation had sent him flying up the stairs. Now all these impulses had gone, and he was just frightened.

Knife me, push me over, or both, Argyll thought. Spoiled for choice. Probably push me over, he decided. More ambiguous.

An arm went round his neck, pushing him back so his head rested on the parapet wall. He saw the flash of the knife in the moonlight. He was choking. He grabbed the wrist below the knife, not that it made any evident difference. The planned resistance was useless; the unplanned response was much more effective: reflex action brought his knee up between the other's legs so fast and so sharply that the impact hurt it. To Argyll's faint astonishment, the grip relaxed as his attacker clutched at the offended area and let out a deep, and very satisfying yelp of pain.

But the respite was only brief. His assailant had kept hold of the knife and was still much too close. Argyll clenched his fist and hit him. He'd never hit anyone before, having led a quiet and largely withdrawn childhood in a world which disapproved of shows of temper among the young. He should have got into more fights when he was small. It was odd how small his fists felt, and how much his knuckles hurt when he punched the man in the general area of the chin. He made a few more desultory taps, then stopped. He could do no more and it didn't seem to be much use in the long run anyway. His assailant, at least, also seemed less than happy after his brief contact with Argyll's knee. They both paused, breathing heavily and looking at each other, eyes less than a foot apart. In the dim light, Argyll saw his face clearly for the first time, and was briefly shocked into inactivity.

Then the knife hand swung back for the last time, and Argyll reached into his pocket for his last weapon. A pity he hadn't thought of it before. He aimed the aerosol, and pressed the button.

There was a scream of agony, the knife clattered to the stone flagging. Argyll was appalled. He hadn't even considered what he'd been doing, just grabbed the one faint chance the moment it occurred to him. He backed away, and stood, dumbly, watching the torment he'd just caused.

One hand still trying to rub the acid out of his eyes, Argyll's assailant was scrabbling in the pocket of a heavy blue jacket.

Oh, Christ, not a gun as well, Argyll thought. This man's a walking bloody arsenal. It was no good even thinking of another round of fighting to try and disarm him. There was no strength left for that. With the certainty that only desperation can provide, Argyll ran forward once more and pushed with every drop of muscle-power and will-power he had left.

Without a scream, a cry, or any noise at all, Antonio Ferraro, deputy director of the Italian National Museum, disappeared over the edge and hurtled to the ground, three hundred feet below.

14

ARGYLL sat there for twenty minutes, maybe more. He was too exhausted and in too much pain to move. The adrenaline washed out of his system, leaving a barely functioning wreck behind it. It was very quiet, now. His back resting against the parapet wall, he looked upwards, beyond the tall bell tower that rose from the middle of the Campanile, and stared at the stars. It wasn't really appropriate but he was far too washed out to do anything else. Flavia was, at the least, badly injured and might well be lying down there with her throat cut. He had, it seemed, just killed someone who would, knowing his current run of luck, turn out to be entirely innocent of any wrongdoing. All for that stupid, useless picture. The thought made him feel ill. It would have been better if he'd never heard of bloody Mantini.

Great. A good evening. Why can't you do something right for once? he asked himself bitterly. That's what comes of trying to be so clever. It'll take a lot of explaining this time. And the police will be all over the place soon.

They were evidently all over the place already. He heard sirens as cars drove into the Campo; shouted orders. Footsteps coming up the stairs. Oh well, he thought listlessly, here we go.

What happened next didn't really concern him much; he still ached and that seemed more important. He didn't even take his eyes off the sky when a couple of people came through the door and walked over to him.

A flashlight shone in his face, blinding him. He shut his eyes, and heard General Bottando say: "It's Argyll. He's still alive."

THE rest of the night passed in a blur. Once Argyll realised he wasn't going to be instantly carted off to the local lockup, he had thrown a fit, refusing to let a doctor anywhere near him until he was told about Flavia. They said she was all right, but he refused to believe them.

Eventually, two policemen had to carry him down so he could see for himself. It was difficult, and with much cursing, they tried to help him down the steps without letting him fall. As far as Argyll was concerned, it was well worth it. Flavia was sitting against the wall, wrapped in a blanket, her head covered with a large bandage. A small spot of red was just visible around her left temple.

She was conscious, complaining of a headache, and asking for some food. There was clearly not much wrong with her. Argyll was so pleased, so relieved and so exhausted, all he could do was pat her hand and look at her. Bottando stood over them with his arms crossed and looked disapproving.

"General, what about the picture, is it safe?" Flavia asked drowsily. She had been given a sleeping draught which was nearly taking effect.

He nodded. "Yup," he said. "Cut out of its frame and damaged, but still basically in one piece. It'll be all right after a bit of work."

This contented her, and she fell asleep. It was the moment for Argyll to say something, but he couldn't be bothered. It could all wait until tomorrow.

"Young man, she's fast asleep. If you would let go of her hand and stop staring like a lovesick cow, perhaps we could bandage up that arm of yours."

Argyll hadn't even noticed, but he must have scraped his arm on the coarse, abrasive stone as he ran up the stairs. Now he did notice it and it hurt abominably. He stuck it out, and the doctor began washing and dressing it.

"What happened up there, anyway? How did he fall off?" Bottando asked.

"I pushed him. But it really wasn't my fault."

"Yes, yes, we know all that," Bottando said impatiently. "But why did you push him?"

"He attacked Flavia and came after me. He was pulling a gun. It was the only thing I could think of."

"I see. And he just stood there and let you give him a shove?" Argyll didn't like the tone of that. Didn't seem entirely sympathetic.

"I doubt that he saw me coming." Argyll pulled the little aerosol tube out of his pocket. "I sprayed this in his face while we were fighting. It's a cleaning solution for paintings."

"Ah. That'll probably explain it. Needed to clean out his eyes a lot, I imagine. I sympathise with your caution, but he wasn't pulling a gun." Bottando looked at him with a weak smile. "He didn't have one. I'm afraid you have pushed him off a three-hundred-foot tower because he was reaching for a handkerchief."

THE news upset him considerably, but not for long. He was also given a sleeping shot, and drifted off thinking how wonderful Flavia was. Which was generous, he thought, considering how badly she'd treated him. Like everyone else. A cruel and unjust world, when he was only trying to help.

Both of them slept deeply and soundly, even though much of the time was spent in the back of two police cars whistling back down the autostrada to Rome. They didn't even wake when they were lifted bodily from the cars and carried like sacks of turnips up the stairs to Flavia's flat.

Bottando supervised the operation, clucking over them

with concern. As Flavia had only one bed, he wondered briefly where to deposit Argyll. But there was nothing for it: he conquered his prejudices and had the Englishman laid elegantly by her side, hoping she would understand it was an emergency measure and wouldn't protest too much the next day. That accomplished, he gave instructions to the policeman who was settling into Flavia's armchair that he was to remain until they woke, then bring them to the office as quickly as possible.

Flavia woke first, coming out of a drugged sleep so slowly she wasn't even aware of doing so. Argyll was curled up beside her, his hand holding on to her arm. She stroked his hair absentmindedly, wondering where she'd put the aspirin.

Then she remembered, began to resent his presence, stopped the display of affection and poked him violently on the arm. "What are you doing here?" she asked.

"Jesus. Be careful. That's tender." He woke up fast, shut his eyes again, then opened them and peered around. "This is your bed, isn't it?"

"Yes. I'll get some coffee. Then we can work out why you're in it." Flavia crawled out of bed and headed out the door to the kitchen. She came back in immediately and grabbed her dressing gown. "There's a policeman out there," she observed. She nodded good morning to him on her second entrance and waved him into silence when he began to explain his presence. "Not yet. Can't take it."

She leaned heavily on the kitchen counter while she was waiting for the espresso pot to do its stuff. Her picture of the previous night's events was hazy, but enough to realise it had been a mixed achievement. Argyll had done his bit and found the picture, which went some way to repairing the damage caused by his rather bizarre behaviour in London. Then he had gone and spoiled it by pushing someone off the parapet. She should be grateful, she supposed, but still wished he hadn't.

When Argyll emerged from the bedroom, he was clearly in no more rosy a mood. His arm hurt, his stomach hurt, his lungs hurt, his legs hurt. He was also brooding over his performance. All that risk, that appalling danger, and for what? She could easily be lying in a little plastic bag with a label round her toe. So could he, for that matter. And not even a Raphael, fine painter though he was, was worth that. Too fast. Rush, rush, rush. That had always been his great trouble. Not enough attention to detail.

So they sat in companionable misery until the policeman, a veritable youth who had recently joined the force and who wasn't sure how to proceed in these circumstances, interrupted and, following orders, tried to escort them to the office. Flavia made short work of him, and he departed on his own, carrying a message that they'd be along in an hour.

They spent it having showers, eating breakfast, discussing the events of the night before and staring out of the window. If there had been any chance of Flavia persuading herself into a good humour, it evaporated slowly. Eventually she stood up, tipped the dirty dishes into the sink and turned to Argyll.

"Can't delay it any longer, I guess. We'd better go in and get it over with."

So they walked, as slowly as possible, to the office. "I'm not looking forward to this at all," Argyll commented on the way.

"What are you worried about? All he can do is shout at you. Me, he's going to fire." She had a point.

"But I'm the one who's lost his scholarship," he replied. He had a point too.

Bottando's greeting, though, was a pleasant surprise. "Come in, come in," he said after they had knocked tentatively on his door. "Good of you to come so early." It was a little after noon. Flavia couldn't decide if he was being sarcastic.

"I had a dreadful night last night. You shouldn't go about worrying me like that. Can you imagine how bad I would have felt if you'd got yourselves killed? Apart from the difficulties of explaining to the minister and getting a suitable replacement for you."

"Listen, General, I'm sorry . . ."

He waved her attempts aside. "Don't apologise. I feel bad enough already. These things happen. Of course, it's a pity about the business with the tower, Argyll. But I'm sure you didn't have much choice. Dreadful mess, he made. I'm a little surprised it wasn't you splattered all over the Campo, though. He was much bigger than you."

Argyll confessed that he was equally surprised.

"Ah, well. I don't suppose it will make any difference in the long run. How are you both? Feeling better yet?"

Flavia said they were. Bottando seemed in a remarkably jolly mood. But then he didn't know everything yet.

"Good," he continued, blithely unaware of the depressed state of his assistant. "I'm glad to hear it. In that case you can come along with me while I make my report to the director. I've given him a potted report, but he wants details. I fear he's not at all happy about Ferraro—the death rate in the museum is a little high, these days. Still, that's his problem."

As he led the way to his official police car and they all three squeezed in the back, Argyll was feeling uneasy.

"Are you sure you want me to come along? After all, I can't see Tommaso exactly welcoming me with open arms . . ."

"Probably not," Bottando replied. "No, indeed. You're responsible for nearly all his troubles, I suppose. If you hadn't leapt to the wrong conclusion to start off with, none of this would have happened. But don't worry. I'll protect you."

Driving up the Corso to the museum the conversation became muted, apart from Bottando muttering to himself: "Another Raphael, dio mio! A fine achievement . . ."

"Thank you . . ." began Argyll.

Bottando held up his hand. "Please don't. We can celebrate later. It's the grand picture we must concentrate on at the moment."

For the rest of the journey through the clogged streets of Rome he kept quiet, but Flavia could see in the reflection from the window that he would smile occasionally as he looked absently at the people in the streets. "General, what about Ferraro?" she asked. "I mean, I don't understand how he did it."

Bottando patted her in a fatherly sort of way. "Too much running around, not enough thought, that's the trouble with you young things. I shall tell you when we see the director."

At the museum, the driver opened the rear door to let them out and saluted as they walked up the wide steps to the entrance. Then they strode quickly through the galleries, up some back stairs into the office leading to the director's studio.

"I'm afraid you can't see the director. He's busy."

Bottando searched out his most ferocious expression and put it on. "Nonsense, woman," he told the secretary. "Of course he wants to see me."

"But he's in a very important meeting . . ." she protested as he brushed past and opened the door.

Even someone like Argyll—who was not normally particularly perceptive over matters like the finer nuances of atmosphere—could tell that the mood in the room was not especially happy. Tense, in fact. Which was not surprising, really, as the only occupants, sitting in silence round an unlit coal fire, were the director, Enrico Spello and Sir Edward Byrnes. Clearly, their entry did not interrupt a lively conversation.

"Gentlemen. Good morning. I'm so glad you're all here enjoying yourselves." Bottando rubbed his hands together, his cheerfulness not even dented by the less than amicable air in the room. With exaggerated punctiliousness he introduced everyone, even though they had all met before. He sat down and beamed at the assembled group.

"Well, director, there are many details to go through. First, as you know, the museum now has a replacement Raphael, and we can officially call the first one a fake."

Tommaso nodded. "That is a consolation. A shocking business all round. Ferraro of all people." He shook his head in a gesture which seemed more sorrowful than angry.

"Indeed. A distressing affair. As is the other transaction I have to perform."

"Which is?" Tommaso enquired.

Bottando fished around in his pocket and drew out a piece of paper, glancing around at the other five people in the room as he did so. "It's just a little arrest warrant," he began in an apologetic tone of voice, clearly enjoying himself. He coughed to clear his throat so as not to stumble as he read out the legal phrasing. He always liked to get these little ceremonies right.

"Cavaliere Marco di Tommaso, I have here a warrant to arrest you on charges of conspiracy to defraud the state, conspiracy to commit forgery, conspiracy to pervert the course of justice, and non-declaration of income to the appropriate fiscal authorities."

15

THEY sat in Bottando's office, drinking coffee. Byrnes and Spello had occupied the only comfortable chairs, Flavia and Argyll perched on two tubular-metal affairs brought in for the occasion. Bottando sat at his desk, a look of radiant self-satisfaction about him, Byrnes and Spello had a neutral look on their faces, while Argyll and Flavia brought up the rear with an air of scarcely dissipated anxiety, slowly mingling with a degree of relief.

"Well, well. What a business. The look on the director's face when I read out that warrant was worth a small fortune. I never thought anybody could have spluttered so much," Bottando said with a happy smile on his face. "Couldn't have been better. I was particularly proud of getting him on his income tax. I shall greatly enjoy reading the papers tomorrow. One month before the budget submissions have to go in for next year. I think I'll take the opportunity to add on twenty per cent extra for wages and claim another five assistants. Probably get them now."

"I found it all rather alarming," commented Argyll. "I suppose you were bluffing. But what would you have done if he hadn't started confessing to everything? You would have been in a right mess then."

"Good heavens, young man, what do you take me for? Just because I'm a shade overweight and can't go running around Europe like a runaway train doesn't mean I'm completely senile, you know. Of course I wasn't bluffing: I would have been much more circumspect if you hadn't so brilliantly found that painting. Without that we wouldn't have been able to prove anything."

He smiled at the Englishman's look of blushing modesty.

"It was obvious that it was him. But you were so concerned to slam poor Sir Edward behind bars you ignored the evidence. While I, sitting quietly in my office with calm detachment, could see it all."

"Has anyone ever told you that you're really objectionable when you're smug?" Argyll asked.

"I know. But it's not often I have such a good day. Please forgive me."

"You were about to say why it was obvious."

"Yes. Firstly there was the problem of who knew about

the picture in advance of Argyll's intemperate outburst here after his arrest. And you said you had informed only your supervisor, and that anyway he had been away on sabbatical in Tuscany. Right? And he wrote you a letter telling you he had been reading your paper and had written recommending that you be kept on at your university. He was staying with a friend east of Montepulciano. Interesting, eh?"

Flavia and Argyll leaned back in their chairs, folded their arms simultaneously, and looked exasperated.

"Well. And you remember I told you—I told Flavia anyway—that Tommaso had surprised me by saying he was going to retire next year to Tuscany. A villa outside Pienza, in fact. Ever been there? No? You really should. Very pretty town. A little jewel, in fact. It's very easy to get to: go to Montepulciano and keep on going a few miles east and you're there.

"And it seemed unlikely," Bottando continued, staring at the ceiling, "that two such eminent artistic types should be within spitting distance of each other without meeting. A brief phone call confirmed it. Your supervisor had been staying with Tommaso while he read the paper.

"So that's piece number one. Tommaso had the chance, at least, of knowing about that picture long enough in advance to get a forgery made. I couldn't find any way that Sir Edward might have known. Tommaso investigates, and discovers you're wrong. But he also goes through the evidence and realises that, although there is nothing under there, there should be. You said the same yourself. If someone uncovered the painting and found what looked like a Raphael, they would be predisposed to believe it was genuine.

"But he's no fool. You can't produce any old rubbish and expect to have it accepted. He needed an expert. And who does he think of? Why, good old Professor Morneau, the man who taught him all about painting when he was an art student in Lyons. He found the right man: Morneau was really good. He bought that old painting and used the others for practice. Then he cleaned off the central portion and painted a Raphael, along the lines you've described. Put the fake Mantini on top, dirtied and aged it, switched the pictures when no one was looking. Exit Morneau.

"Of course, I was just a little suspicious of Tommaso anyway, but I couldn't see my way past the fact that Byrnes was the most likely beneficiary, and that the director had a cast-iron alibi on every occasion. Flavia's view that Byrnes had probably been his own employer seemed most likely.

"Things really started crystallising when Byrnes rang me up, a little hot under the collar after Argyll had effectively told him that we knew the picture was a fraud, and that he was going to have to refund all the money." He paused and turned to the Englishman. "Why did you do that, by the way?"

Flavia looked at Argyll disapprovingly, and he looked sheepish again. "As I told Flavia, it seemed a good idea at the time. The idea was that Sir Edward would rush out to Siena, try to destroy the picture, and would get himself arrested. I suppose I owe you an apology," he said to Byrnes, who acknowledged it graciously.

"Very good idea," said Bottando with approval, surprising both Flavia and Argyll almost equally. "Wrong man, of course, but sound in principle. As you know, it was the same sort of plan as the one I adopted.

"In fact," he continued, resuming his monologue, "it was just as well you did go and see him. It was he who pointed out to me that Tommaso had been Morneau's pupil. Until that point, the only person I could see burning the picture and killing Manzoni was Argyll, which implicated Byrnes as I didn't think Argyll was able to think of the fake."

"Thank you very much," said Argyll.

"No offence. I was merely referring to your lack of experience. But you could kill someone; I couldn't see any of these slightly overweight—my apologies, gentlemen—aesthetes taking on Manzoni in a fight. So I reached a stalemate."

Bottando twisted off the cap of a bottle of fizzy mineral water and poured a glass for himself, then offered it round to his audience. "So. Byrnes is commissioned, buys the picture and takes it home, and the fraud is all set. Tommaso had also prepared his end by getting the minister to agree in advance that, should such an opportunity arise, they should leap in and save the Italian heritage.

"The museum buys the picture and Tommaso has the opportunity of directing his tests to the area he knew would pass. He calls Byrnes and gives directions that only the left-hand side of the picture is to be examined. Unfortunately, his secretary overheard the conversation, and told me about it yesterday morning when I was waiting outside his office to see him. It's the penalty for not seeing visitors promptly.

"Then Flavia goes to England and Argyll mentions his bit of evidence. I tell the director what Argyll suspects, and he explodes. But he doesn't do anything. It was only when I tried to get out of going to that party by telling Ferraro I was off to Switzerland in search of some icons, that the picture got wrecked. At this point matters get taken out of Tommaso's hands.

"That was another curiosity that fitted into place when you began to see Tommaso as a possible instigator. All of a sudden he names Ferraro as his successor and says he's going to retire. Odd, that, to do such a favour for someone you clearly and obviously disliked. I suspect that Ferraro found out what was going on when he ran the museum during Tommaso's and Spello's absence. The director said this was when Ferraro effectively clinched the job. I thought it was because he'd done so well, but it was more likely that it was because he'd then got his hold on Tommaso.

"Ferraro goes along and says he knows that I am about to prove the picture was a fake. He names his terms for dealing with the situation and not telling the police. Tommaso has no choice. He agrees and Ferraro, a very much more ruthless person, goes into action.

"Ferraro was in a difficult position. If the forgery survived and was unmasked, Tommaso's reputation and his own chances of becoming director would be damaged. But if it was destroyed and no one proved it was a fake, then Tommaso would again be damaged by the failure to protect a masterpiece.

"Unless of course, the blame could be shifted. Clearly a man who thought ahead. Hence, the rapid appearance of stories in the newspapers about the lapses of the security committee. It pushed Spello into the limelight as a suspect and made me a potential scapegoat. Once I stopped seeing it as a piece of bureaucratic politics and began to look at it as an aspect of the case, then the mist began to clear a bit.

"There were two final weak spots in their defence. Firstly, someone would see how the forgery was done. Manzoni works it out. He tells Ferraro, hoping to secure his position in the museum. Ferraro slips out of the office, murders him, and slips back to work afterwards, leaving late in the evening and making sure the doorman sees him go. The final detail was destroying the original picture, and this, fortunately, is where he slipped up.

"Now we all know what happened, of course, it is easy to see where we went wrong. We had the tendency to assume that the burning of the picture and the knifing of Manzoni were all done by the same person as was behind the fraud. And as Tommaso had a perfect alibi for the murder and for the burning, I couldn't see how he could be responsible."

Flavia objected here. "But Ferraro also had an alibi for when the picture was burnt. You told me so yourself."

"True. Tommaso provided the alibi and the Americans provided an alibi for Tommaso. What we didn't have was an American alibi for Ferraro. Until yesterday, when I rang them again and they said he'd left the director's office halfway through their meeting about the donation. I should have thought of that, as well, because I saw him at the party ten minutes before Tommaso reappeared."

He paused for a few moments to pick up his monologue where he'd left it. "But that was only two days ago. I'm a bit slow. After Byrnes had called and everything began to fall into place, I had a dreadful day. I knew, but had no proof. So I had to take an anguished decision. You were going to Siena. Now, did I tell Ferraro? If I didn't, we'd have proof of the fake, but not of the instigator or the murderer.

"But if I did, Ferraro would inevitably turn up there, and try and destroy all the evidence once and for all. As that could well include you two as well as the picture, I was decidedly nervous.

"Very anguishing indeed. But Sir Edward persuaded me that if we saturated Siena with enough plainclothesmen we could protect you. So, essentially, I adopted the same plan as Argyll, only with a different target. I came up by helicopter to supervise, set up my headquarters in a hotel—not nearly as good as the luxurious effort you two chose, but I'm only a humble policeman—and off we went.

"And we could have protected you, if you hadn't pulled that silly stunt of hiding in the toilets. Novel, but ridiculous. We were convinced you'd come out of the museum and we'd lost you. General panic. We scattered our forces and scoured the streets. And all the restaurants, of course. Nothing. I was convinced you were lying with your throats cut in some dark alley. The worry nearly set off my ulcer again.

"We found you, but only when Ferraro dropped off the tower. He landed a few feet away from a policeman we had watching the Campo for suspicious behaviour—he thought this qualified, and called me.

"No one had noticed him knock on the back door where the night porter hangs out, cosh the poor man and go in. That was because we were so busy wondering where you were. So that's the tale. Ferraro happily out of the way for ever, Tommaso under lock and key."

"What happens now?" asked Argyll. "What's he been charged with?"

"Oh, it doesn't work like that at all. Preventative incarceration first. That's to stop him hot-footing it to Argentina like all the other mobsters. He'll be locked up for, oh, about eighteen months while the prosecutor assembles the case. Then he'll be given a fair trial and found guilty. Lord only knows why it takes that long. It'll be a lovely trial."

Argyll stuck his hand up, tentatively, like a schoolboy wanting to go to the toilet, but had no chance to speak. Flavia got there first.

"I still don't really see why he bothered. After all, he was well off, had a wonderful job, highly envied and admired. Why throw a stunt like this?"

"Ah, well, that was what put me on to him in the first place. For the last six months or so everyone has been telling me how rich the man was. But it occurred to me, when I actually thought about it, that I'd never heard of this legendary wealth before. And I didn't think Tommaso was the sort of person to keep a fact like that to himself.

"So I spent some time looking through the dossiers and my old cases. A very useful exercise. And discovered that, as is often the case, he was christened with his mother's maiden name: Marco. The family was involved in a financial scandal I helped crack in my youth; it went bankrupt as a result. The young Tommaso was plunged suddenly from great wealth into abject poverty, which may have created a sense of greed and desire for revenge. He had no money at all. Not, at least, until he got his hands on the proceeds of this operation. Only then did tales of his wealth begin to circulate."

Byrnes stirred himself in his armchair by the fireplace, and spoke for the first time. "There is also my role in the affair," he began. "I imagine he would have gone ahead anyway, but luring me into the net made the triumph complete. He knew I would be the prime suspect.

"I told you of the Correggio affair. I took the painting back, which I gather made me more suspect. But I took it back when I needn't have because I was convinced it was genuine. I did research, proved it, and eventually sold it for more than Tommaso had paid. He resigned from Treviso for no reason at all aside from the criticism and doubts of a few connoisseurs.

"That rankled, and I can't say I blame him. He also resented me because I'd proved him wrong twice. When this opportunity came up, he took it. This time, he wanted to ridicule all those colleagues who had scorned him. The longer the fraud went on, the more articles and books would be written, and the more scholars would commit themselves. And eventually, possibly in his will so he wouldn't have to give any money back, he would reveal all and make a laughingstock of them.

"But this new evidence turns up, largely because Argyll sowed his first seeds of doubt, Morneau dies unexpectedly, and Ferraro takes the matter out of his hands. The whole thing stopped being an ingenious and well-conceived joke and turned nasty. A great pity. In some ways I rather wish he had got away with it. On the other hand, we do at least now have a real Raphael."

Argyll shook his head. "Ah, well, now then. I'm afraid not. I've been trying to tell you ever since we got here. I think I goofed again . . ."

There was a pause, followed by a quiet groan from the others in the room as it dawned on them what he had said. Only Flavia, who'd been waiting for this all afternoon, looked relieved that he'd finally got around to it.

"Again?" Bottando raised his eyebrows. "A second time? Another mistake? But Flavia said you'd found it. You told her there was a painting underneath."

Argyll smiled a little shamefacedly. " 'Painting,' not 'a painting.' There was. Green. Light-green paint. That's what I told her. But I was just about to explain when she was bopped on the head that it was a bad sign, not a good one. All painters use a dead colour to prepare the canvas in some way. Generally it's a sort of off-white. But Mantini used light green. That's what I was trying to say. It was a genuine Mantini from top to bottom. There was nothing underneath at all. I got the wrong picture."

There was a brief moment while everyone in the room looked at him sadly. Argyll felt like an insect.

"This really is very careless of you," Bottando said heavily. "I went in to Tommaso because I thought we had clear and absolute proof at last that the first painting was a fake. Think what would have happened if he had sat there and denied it all. We couldn't have touched him. You have now misidentified two Raphaels in the space of a year. Probably a record."

"I know," Argyll said sadly. "And I'm dreadfully sorry about it. All I can say is that it should have been the right one, they both should, in fact. I really can't understand it. I must have missed something. Third time lucky, d'you think?"

"No. Absolutely not. Forget it. Even if you found the right one no one would believe you any more. You just concentrate on Mantini, that can't cause any turmoil. And do be a bit more reticent about this sort of thing in future."

• • •

IN the months afterwards, Argyll followed the General's advice and made steady progress in the task of restoring Carlo Mantini to his proper place in the artistic pantheon. His sudden and extraordinary dedication was not entirely due to a sense of scholarship, however. Byrnes had forgiven Argyll for entertaining the idea that he was a murderer, but he was quietly putting on the pressure for something to show for the fellowship. He also made a vague offer of a job in his Rome gallery once the dissertation was finished.

With the possibility of permanent residence in Italy to motivate him, Argyll slaved away at the Hertziana, the German art library at the top of the Spanish steps. Surrounded by the books he needed, and with a major incentive to work, he had little excuse not to. Flavia also bullied him mercilessly, while always reminding him that it was for his own good. By and large he agreed, and it caused no rupture in the close and companionable friendship that was slowly growing up between them, despite their differences in character.

His work was not especially exciting, but it was none too demanding either. He would put in a few hours in the morning, have a leisurely lunch at the Press Club, then return home to sit, hammering away at his typewriter. It all came out slowly and painfully, and he spent many an hour staring at the wall, searching for inspiration or, failing that, at least the will-power to get on with it. He fixed a photograph of the fake Raphael opposite where he sat: no matter what its origins, he still thought it a wonderful picture. Next to it he pinned the old copy Morneau had used as a base. Beauty and the beast. It reminded him of the whole business. Looking back, it all seemed like quite a good time.

Slowly, he made progress, but got bogged down in the central chapter—which dealt with the fraud—as he tried to find something new to say. And he'd agreed to give a paper at an art history conference in January—that would slow things down as well, especially as he could think of nothing to talk about. It would also require a trip to England at the worst possible time of year, but there was no way he could get out of it now.

Thus Argyll thought as he lay on the bed staring at the wall, cigarette in hand, taking a breather. Typing gives you a sore back. He looked at his two pictures again. The copy was indeed an awful thing. Who would ever wear such ostentatious and crude jewellery, even in the sixteenth century? Such a bizarre design, as well. A ring made of dead birds, indeed.

He walked around the room and thought, clarifying matters as an idea for his paper began to crystallise in his mind. It was going to need a lot of work, but that was fairly easy once you knew the general outline.

He was tempted to abandon his typewriter for the rest of the afternoon, amble off into the fading autumn light to see Flavia and tell her the outline. But he abandoned the notion. Flavia was a patient girl, but not that much of a saint. She would merely criticise him for not getting on with the thesis. Besides, she worked hard, and he didn't want to interrupt her.

So he kept quiet and worked discreetly on the side, accumulating the odd spots of information here and there. It was hard, but came in little drips until he had enough to throw a bit of his recently adopted caution aside. In late November, he went to London, where he saw Byrnes about his forthcoming job. His benefactor was most accomodating. A nice man, when you got to know him. Sense of humour, too. He also dug out Phil, and twisted his arm until he agreed to invite him to lunch with his father at the National Trust. Out of this meeting came an invitation to go north for a long weekend in the freezing cold of a Yorkshire October. Then he came back to Rome.

Flavia was amazed by his behaviour. He had begun working on his dissertation but was clearly not consumed by it. Now, to write a mere twenty-minute paper for the conference, he was working like a demon. Long hours, late into the night, writing, rewriting, and footnoting. He also refused to let her see what he'd written, despite her offers to check it through. She could hear it at the conference, he told her, if she wanted to come.

16

ARGYLL was very nervous, not having given many papers before, and certainly not in front of such a large audience. "There must be about two hundred people here, even though some are leaving for tea. A couple of paragraphs of this and they'll sit down again," he thought as he walked to the podium.

He took out his paper and looked around, waiting for the hum of chattering art historians to die away. This might be fun. Certainly, the previous offering had not been much competition. This lot were about to get the shock of their lives. He spied his flatmate Rudolf Beckett, sitting morosely in one of the back seats, and gave him a little wave. The poor man had been persuaded to come along, and was clearly regretting the atypical gesture of friendship.

"In the past few months," Argyll began, "there has been a great deal of discussion, in journals and in more popular papers [polite laughter] about the purchase of a supposed Raphael by the forger Jean-Luc Morneau. As you all know, the former director of the Museo Nazionale in Rome will shortly stand trial for complicity in the affiar. I shall not, therefore, deal with this aspect of the business for fear of contravening Italian restrictions and in case anything I say prejudices Dottore Tommaso's chance of a fair trial.

"Rather, today, I would like to go back to the original proposition which started the whole sequence of events off. That is the evidence that a painting by Raphael of Elisabetta di Laguna, once owned by the di Parma family, was indeed painted over by Carlo Mantini to get it through Papal customs and to England. Because of the publicity surrounding the exposure of the forgery, the question of the original has rather been lost sight of, even though it undoubtedly existed. I intend to demonstrate that evidence exists to prove conclusively the last destination of the picture."

There was a little stir in the audience. No more chattering from dissidents at the back now. The tea-trolley brigade was settling down nicely into their seats. It was true that Argyll had sacrificed something of scholarly rigour for the sake of maximum impact, but it could hardly fail. Compared with papers on "Manet's Conception of Human Progress," or "Theorising the Male Gaze," this was rock and roll.

"It has always been assumed that the painting disappeared either because it never left Italy, or because the dealer Samuel Paris absconded with it at some stage." Well, *he* had assumed that, anyway. But there was no harm in generalising a bit.

"The main evidence for this was that the Earl of Clomorton died of a heart attack the moment the Mantini arrived in England. A notoriously stingy man, it was assumed that realising he had been robbed of more than seven hundred pounds was too much for him.

"A letter from his wife, however, brings this interpretation into question." He read through the letter he had shown to Flavia in his flat. "This clearly states that Clomorton was expected in Yorkshire and had been in London with Samuel Paris for three weeks 'fussing over the consignment.' He died a week after this letter was written.

"A second letter from her brother appears to reassure his widow that unkind gossip about the fraud will never come out." He read out the document from the newspaper cutting he had taken. Not scholarly, but he had checked that it was an accurate transcription of the original. "Again, this reading is problematic. I find it unlikely that anyone, in possession of a Raphael, would wait for three weeks before looking at it. Paris was on hand, and he was a cleaner as well as a dealer. Surely it is more likely that he would have set to work the moment the picture was unloaded from the boat? And if that is the case, whatever lay under the Mantini would have been discovered within a matter of hours.

"So what did the Earl die of? It is scarcely conceivable that a man, however mean, would die of shock at being robbed a whole three weeks after the shock was administered. Moreover, Clomorton was buried in Yorkshire. He died in January, the month when English roads were at their most impassable. And he died on the date when his wife was expecting him to arrive home. If his death was caused by a shock received in the restorer's studio, would his family really have bothered to cart his body nearly three hundred miles at that time of year?

"So let us return to Lady Arabella." Here, he gave the extracts from Viscount Perceval's diary he had read to Flavia. "Perhaps this should be seen in a new light," he continued. "When Perceval referred to the 'dark-haired beauty' Clomorton said he was going to bring to Yorkshire, he was not referring to some mistress he had picked up. The phrase, after all, could refer to a painting of Elisabetta di Laguna. However, it was unfortunate that he made his little jest to the Duchess of Albemarle, who misinterpreted it and immediately wrote a warning to his wife. She naturally feared her husband was back at his old tricks and was outraged by yet another affront to her honour. She was, after all, a woman with a terrible temper. She had publicly assaulted her first husband and cheerfully confessed to threatening the second.

"So we have a possible solution. The Earl arrives home, complete with his latest consignment of pictures and excited at the prospect of showing them off. He does not get the welcome he expects. There is a blazing row, Lady A's temper gets the better of her and she lashes out. But this time she goes too far, and she kills him. This is what her brother referred to in his letters. Not keeping the fraud secret, but keeping the murder secret. It was put out that the Earl had died of a heart attack, and he was quietly and rapidly buried in the family vaults. I was present when the tomb, now the responsibility of the National Trust, was opened a few weeks ago. The Earl's skull was cracked, a symptom rarely associated with heart failure."

Another rumble from the audience, like a mass attack of indigestion. Argyll paused to let it subside, and winked at Flavia in the front row. He straightened his face to deliver the knockout.

"So what next? Lady Arabella has already delivered her opinion about her husband's pictures, and what she wanted to do with them. Copies and impositions that should be hidden away. This is exactly what happens, and they have stayed there, for the most part, ever since. Those that weren't sold before the family vacated the premises in the 1940s are still in their original positions, in lesser bedrooms, down dark corridors or in the cellars."

He paused for maximum effect. He'd been practising for days. "According to surviving inventories, Raphael's picture of Elisabetta di Laguna—bought by the Earl, painted over by Mantini, uncovered and delivered in good faith by Samuel Paris—hung just outside the staff entrance to the kitchens, its true worth entirely unrecognised. It rested there, being splattered with gravy from passing trolleys, caked with smoke and covered with spilt coffee, for more than two hundred years. Its condition by the time it was sold at Christie's in 1947 was dreadful."

Argyll had once heard a psychiatrist analyse the speeches of successful politicians. The man had explained that many of them, to create an air of excitement, persuade the audience to clap; then shout the next few lines of the speech over the applause, thus creating an impression of spellbinding oratory. He had wanted to try this for years. His statement about the gravy caused a respectable stir, so he raised his voice and ploughed on.

"From here on tracing the picture is a routine matter of provenance work."

They calmed down a bit, so he paused, took a sip from his glass of water, and let them wait. Of all his discoveries of the past year—and he was the first to admit that some had proven embarrassingly below par—he was the most proud of this one. It called for observation, intuition and imagination, the sort of things he normally wasn't very good at. This proved he could do it when he tried.

"At the 1947 sale, the picture was bought by one Robert MacWilliam, a Scottish doctor. He died in 1972 and it was sold at Parson's in Edinburgh, for two hundred and twenty-five guineas, to none other than Sir Edward Byrnes."

A hushed silence at this, as they wondered what horrendous revelation came next. "When I informed him of this, Sir Edward was greatly gratified. At any one stage I was afraid he might die of laughter. When he recovered and thought back, he informed me that he had never suspected that the picture was of any value at all. Indeed, he had not even bothered to have it cleaned. Someone came into his gallery one day, offered a price that gave him a small profit, and he accepted. After some searching, he found the record. The picture had been bought by a small private collector on the Continent. It remained in this collection until he also died a few years back.

"Now we come to the final stage, and I must apologise to you for delaying so long. The Raphael affair has been embarrassing all round. Technicians, in particular, are still upset by the fact that they didn't notice the fraud perpetrated on them. Raphael painted in a particular way, and they feel they should have noticed something wrong. I expect there can be few in this audience who do not know the process by which Jean-Luc Morneau created his fake. To do it required immense skill and sympathy for the painter he was imitating. He used Raphael's techniques, Raphael's recipes for paint mixtures, Raphael's style.

"I hate to have to tell you, but he also used a Raphael. The sale records show that the portrait of Elisabetta di Laguna was sold, as 'portrait of a lady, copy after Fra Bartolommeo' for three thousand Belgian francs, to Jean-Luc Morneau. There is one photograph of it."

The picture Argyll had first seen in a Roman restaurant appeared on the screen. "The critical proof is the left hand," Argyll continued, indicating the area with a little pointer. "You see there is a ring." An even more blurred enlargement flashed up. "It is designed as two entwined pelicans. That, of course, is the symbol of the di Parma family. Elisabetta was the Marchese's mistress, and it was quite in order that she should wear the ring to show to whom she belonged. The liaison, after all, was hardly kept a secret.

"It needs only a brief comparison of the forgery and the original"—two slides flashed up on the screen—"to see the similarities in the backgrounds of the two paintings. That was why the tests failed to reveal that the picture was a fake. The bits examined were very much genuine.

"Morneau needed an authentic Italian canvas of the right period, and some passable paintwork to create the illusion of a real Raphael. It seems that he had better raw material than he could ever have realised. He scored through the accumulated dirt of two centuries, probably with some dilute acid, to prepare the surface for his work. I don't imagine that he ever paid much attention to the original painting that lay underneath the grime. To us, after all, it hardly appears to be the representation of a great beauty. Tastes change. Nearly all of Raphael's work, except this window and parts of the interior against which the figure is framed, was simply erased so that he could paint his fake Raphael on top. As you know, what remained was destroyed, along with Morneau's work, during the attack in the museum."

The result was better than he had hoped. He had expected tumultuous applause, roars of approval, programme notes thrown into the air. He got none of that, but the reaction was still more satisfying. Faced with the stunned amazement of the audience, he folded up his paper and stuffed it into his pocket. Then he clattered noisily down the steps from the podium, his metal-tipped shoes echoing across the silent hall. Flavia was waiting for him, beaming with delight.

"Slow but sure. What a clever thing you are, after all," she said. And kissed him, gently, on the nose.